WITCHES GET STITCHES
A WITCH ON THE ROCKS COZY MYSTERY
BOOK EIGHT

LILY HARPER HART

HARPERHART PUBLICATIONS

Copyright © 2024 by Lily Harper Hart

All rights reserved.

No part of this book may be reproduced in any form or by any electronic or mechanical means, including information storage and retrieval systems, without written permission from the author, except for the use of brief quotations in a book review.

❦ Created with Vellum

1
ONE

Grayson "Gray" Hunter watched his girlfriend, Hali Waverly, take careful steps as they headed up the walkway to one of their favorite restaurants. To an outsider, she probably looked like a normal woman taking in the beautiful view. Maybe meandering a little, but why not? He knew better, though.

Hali's hip surgery was behind them, but she was still going through physical therapy. He helped with that—and found it enjoyable—but she was starting to get impatient. She was a woman who preferred being independent. That meant she didn't want to rely on him for everything. They lived on St. Pete Beach, though, and sand was an unforgiving mistress that constantly wanted to take Hali down. Since Hali's favorite place in the world was the beach, that made life difficult for both of them.

As if she sensed him watching her, Hali lifted her eyes. He automatically smiled—he was truly happy with her recovery—but his mother hen tendencies were always at the ready. If she started to fall, he would catch her. If something started to hurt, he was ready to swoop in and pick her up.

Hali wanted neither of those things. She wanted to do it herself.

"Don't even think about it," she warned in a low voice, as if reading his mind.

"They could at least sweep the sand off the walkway," Gray complained. He kept close to her, but not so close that she would balk. He didn't want a fight. This was their first big dinner out of the villa in weeks, and he wanted it to go perfectly. They'd been forced to eat almost all their meals at Paradise Lodge Golf Course and Resort, which was where Hali's tiki bar and free villa were located. The food there was great—they ate it on the regular of their own free will—but they were both excited to be out and about.

"I'm fine," she assured him. "I'm not going to fall."

"I know." He smiled because it was expected. Inside, his stomach was clenched. She looked tired. She'd worked up a light sheen of sweat just walking from the back of the lot—where she'd insisted they park—to the front of the restaurant. Sure, it was still ninety degrees out with high humidity, but her rehab had been tough for both of them.

Hali finally made it to the front door and let loose a tittering breath. "That wasn't so bad." She didn't sound certain of herself, which frustrated Gray on a different level. She'd stolen his heart with her sharp tongue and independent streak. She still had it of course, but it was hard for him to watch her struggle.

"Maybe we should sit inside," he suggested before thinking it through. "You might prefer the air-conditioning."

Her gaze was dark when it landed on him. "We're sitting on the patio. We always sit on the patio."

"Fine." Gray held up his hands in supplication. "It's just a hot night."

It was indeed a hot night. Even more than normal. Hali would not allow the heat to drag her down, though. Not after how far she'd come.

"It's only a little farther," she said. "I'm sorry it's taking so long. I thought I would be faster now."

"Don't." Gray moved in behind her quickly and pressed his forehead to the back of her head. He hated it when she felt guilty for slowing him down. "I just want a nice dinner. I don't care how long it takes us to get there."

Hali cared, though. She didn't come out and say it, but she most definitely cared. Even when her hip was at its worst before the surgery—a result of being hit by the resort owner when he was out gallivanting around on his cart when drunk—she'd forced herself to go up and down the sand in front of her tiki bar multiple times a day. Despite the pain, she'd managed it ... and had been prepared to keep suffering going forward.

Gray had been the one to talk her into the surgery. He hated seeing her suffer. She'd been afraid—if the surgery didn't work, she was out of options—and had initially resisted. Ultimately, she knew that if she wanted a life where she could chase their future children on the beach, she would have to go through with it.

That didn't mean these past few weeks had been sunshine and roses. She was in pain after the surgery ... and for more reasons than one. Her movement had been limited. She'd had to put her beloved tiki bar in the hands of her brother, Jesse, and Gray's brother, Rusty. Not being able to control everything had turned her into a fraught mess. She was starting to come out the other side, though, and they were both grateful.

It took her another three minutes to navigate out to the patio. She looked relieved when she finally sat. Gray's first instinct was to ask for a bag of ice to press to her recovering hip, but he knew that would mortify her. So, he said nothing and instead sat across from her.

"You can't drink on your meds," he said. "Well, you can't drink a lot. Maybe one margarita wouldn't hurt."

Hali opened her mouth and then shut it, considering. "I think it's best not to risk that," she said finally. "The meds will be done tomorrow. I can wait one more day."

That was another thing Gray was worried about. She was on painkillers, but the prescription was about to run out. He couldn't stand watching her when she was trying to hide her discomfort. He wasn't certain what the following day would bring, but he had no intention of begging trouble the night before. "Okay. Iced tea it is."

"You can have a drink," Hali countered. "I don't want you going without because of me."

He shook his head. "No. I don't need anything. Besides, it's hot. I don't want to become dehydrated."

Hali was naturally suspicious by nature, but she didn't give him a hard time. His head was as hard as hers. When he made up his mind about something, he didn't change it. This would be no different. "Maybe you can have a beer on the patio when we get home."

Gray automatically nodded. "I could do that. We'll just go with the iced tea now." He opened his menu but checked the specials sheet that had been printed out first. "Oh, they have the king crab legs you wanted."

"I'm going to eat my weight in crab," Hali said. "You might have to carry me back to the truck simply because I won't be able to button my shorts."

Gray smirked. She hadn't been able to wear anything

other than drawstring shorts since the surgery. She'd insisted on wearing shorts with a snap for dinner tonight. He'd had to help her into them—something she loathed—but she was stubborn as a mule when she wanted to be.

"You're in luck," he said. "I happen to love carrying you."

"So I've noticed," she said dryly.

"I could carry you down the beach after dinner," he offered. "I mean ... if you want to sit out there." She'd been forced away from the beach for the most part since the surgery. He knew she was chomping at the bit to get back. Unfortunately for her, the doctor had warned her that walking on sand for more than a few steps was still down the road a bit. Sand was uneven, and if she slipped the wrong way, it would be bad. It could cause her to contort and hurt her hip. So, if she wanted to spend time listening to the water—a favorite activity for both of them—she was going to have to accept help.

"Let's see how we feel after we eat, huh?" Hali suggested. "If we walk down the beach, you're going to have to come back for your truck."

"I don't care." It was true. He didn't. "I can manage that tomorrow after I drop you off for work."

Hali cocked an eyebrow. "I'm walking to work tomorrow."

Gray recognized the challenge in her tone and knew she meant what she was saying. "I know you are. Before you decide to get worked up and pick a fight, you should know that I'll be walking with you." *And hanging out for a bit to make sure you don't fatigue yourself,* he silently added.

"I've got it under control, Gray," she insisted. "It's not a long walk to the tiki bar. That's why I have the setup I have."

"You have the setup you have because Franklin Craven

is a complete and total jackhole," Gray replied. Since Franklin was his former uncle, he felt he could say whatever he wanted, whenever he wanted about the man. "He hit you, and rather than go to jail, he decided to pay you off."

"An arrangement I agreed to," she reminded him.

"That's neither here nor there. I still want to punch him whenever I see him."

"I don't think that's only because of me. You disliked him before I came along."

In truth, Gray had trouble remembering his life before Hali came along. They hadn't been together all that long—not in the grand scheme of things at least—but he couldn't imagine living without her now. She'd filled holes he hadn't realized needed filling. When he looked at his future, she was all he saw.

That made him protective and growly when things popped up. Sure, Hali was a witch and could take care of herself, but he would die before he let anything bad happen to her. She'd already been through enough as far as he was concerned. He wanted smooth sailing going forward.

The server came and took their orders. They waited until their drinks were delivered to start talking logistics.

"So, I'm walking you to the tiki bar tomorrow." Gray squared his shoulders and prepared himself for a fight. "I'm also going to be working from there as much as possible in case..." He didn't finish the last part. He thought better of it.

"In case I fall apart and can't run my own bar," Hali said. "Go ahead and say it." She didn't sound angry as much as afraid.

"Baby, I just want to be close to you," Gray countered. It wasn't a lie. It wasn't the whole truth either. "I've gotten used to spending all of my time with you. I'm afraid I'll go through withdrawal if I stop cold turkey."

Hali rolled her eyes at the schmaltz. "Ha, ha."

"It's true." Gray kept going. "I like waking up with you. I like having my breakfast with you. I like showering with you."

"Yes, well, we can't stay joined at the hip." She was firm on that. "We'll kill each other eventually. You're feeling all soft and stuff because you think I'm weak."

"Not weak," he countered, annoyance coming out to play. "I don't think you're weak. In fact, you're the strongest person I know. I *do* think you're vulnerable." He leaned close and lowered his voice. "Also, if you take a step back in your recovery now, it just means we're going to have to start all over. Doesn't it make more sense to be smart about it?"

She sighed but didn't respond. That's how he knew he'd won.

"I'm working at the tiki bar for the entire day tomorrow," he repeated. "I don't think you're going to fall—and I know that's what you're thinking—but I also don't think you'll rest unless I'm there to push you to rest."

"I can rest," Hali said, although she didn't sound all that convincing. "Sometimes."

He smirked. "I plan to be close all of this week. Then we will have a meeting of the minds over the weekend, and I'll adjust so I'm not smothering you."

"You're not smothering me," Hali countered. "I just... I don't want you giving up everything that makes you happy for me."

"Hali, *you* are what makes me happy. You have been since the moment I met you."

Because she recognized he was telling the truth, she forced herself to get back on track. "Let's just get through tomorrow and then we'll talk again. We'll take it on a day-by-day basis."

That was as close to a win as he was going to get, so Gray nodded. "Your brother is still going to be hanging around tomorrow, right?"

Hali frowned at mention of Jesse. Her baby brother had been nothing but a menace since he'd stepped in to help her, to the point where Gray's more forceful brother Rusty had taken charge. Together, they'd managed to keep Hali's bar afloat. Actually, the numbers had been good while they were in charge. That didn't mean Hali didn't want to reclaim her territory.

"He said he would," she replied, evasively averting her gaze.

Gray scowled. "Did you tell him not to show up?"

"I said I would let him know."

"And have you let him know?"

Hali turned back to him. "Have you talked to your mother?"

Now it was Gray's turn to scowl. His mother, Helene Hunter, had entered into an agreement with the dark merrow that had recently been haunting St. Pete Beach. Under that agreement, they were all willing to sacrifice Hali. The merrow had a plan to take over the entire beach. They'd stopped them. Gray wasn't over the betrayal, though. Perhaps if it had just been the one betrayal, he could've gotten over it. It was her second big betrayal, however. The first had been when she essentially shunned him and did nothing as he was kicked out of the pack for standing up for a young teenager who didn't want to be married off to an older shifter. For that, he'd been ostracized ... and his parents had done nothing. They'd recently come back into his life, full of apologies, but one of the first things Helene had done was ally herself with the enemy that wanted to destroy Hali.

Gray was not over it. He didn't think he would ever get over it.

"I know you're mad," Hali started.

"She wanted you dead," Gray replied darkly. "Of course I'm mad."

"She admitted to her mistake, though," Hali argued. "I mean...she knew she did wrong. She could've said nothing and hoped she was never found out, but she didn't do that. She told me what she did, and that allowed us to take down the merrow. They're no longer a threat."

"And you think I should be dancing a jig because of it?" Gray challenged.

"I don't know. We've only ever slow danced. Do you even have rhythm? Because—and I'm not saying this to disparage you—but you don't look like the sort of guy who has rhythm. I think you need rhythm to dance a jig."

Gray ordered himself not to laugh—it would only encourage her—but he couldn't stop himself. "You're lucky you're cute," he said before sipping his iced tea. "As for rhythm, unfortunately, you're right. If you want to stand in my arms as I sway back and forth, I can manage that. I can't twerk or anything though."

A giggle erupted out of Hali. "People haven't been twerking for a decade. How old are you?"

"Old enough to know what I've got and that I want to keep it." Gray poked her side. He sobered when he looked into her eyes and saw she wasn't going to let it go. "You can't decide I'm going to forgive my mother and that's that," he said in a soft voice.

Hali pressed her lips together and nodded. "I don't want to tell you what to feel."

"No, you just don't want this to be the end for my mother and me because you'll always blame yourself for it," Gray said. "The thing is, as much as I don't want you blaming yourself, I also don't want to allow that woman to stay in our lives if she's going to try to hurt you."

"I don't think she'll do that again." Hali was adamant. "She realizes she made a mistake. Can't you give her one more chance?"

"And what if that chance leads to you getting hurt, or worse?"

"It won't."

"You can't know that, Hali."

"I just don't want to be the reason that you don't have a family."

And that was the crux of it, Gray recognized. Hali was close with her family. Even when they irritated her—and that happened often—she loved them. Gray had never been that close with his parents. His brother was another story. Rusty was his best friend—well, other than Hali—and nothing would destroy their bond. His parents were another story.

"I need time to think on it," Gray said. "I know that's hard for you because ... well, just because ... but I can't be forced into a decision on this. Right now, I don't want to see my mother. When I make a permanent decision, I'll let you know."

Hali's sigh was long and drawn out. "Okay."

He arched an eyebrow. This conversation had been a little too easy. "Okay? That's all you're going to say? You're not going to give me a hard time?"

"No, because it's really none of my business."

"That's not true. Everything in my life is your business.

It's just... I don't know how I feel. If I let her stay and she does something else that hurts you, I won't forgive myself."

"Your father wasn't to blame regardless," Hali argued. "You could at least see him."

"My father married that woman," Gray argued. "He might not have been aware this time, but he knows she's hardly trustworthy when she sets her mind to something."

"I just want you to be happy. Now that the merrow are gone, we have nothing but blue skies ahead of us. Well, I mean, once I can walk on the beach without you carrying me. Whenever that is."

He smiled at her dismay. "I happen to like carrying you. I'm going to carry you on the beach after dinner, so you can take a breath." *And I can be with you when you relax,* he silently added. "We're going to spend an hour just decompressing. I don't want you worrying about my mother."

Hali looked as if she wanted to press the issue further, but she didn't. She knew when she'd taken it too far. "I would love to spend some time on the beach with you."

"Good." Gray took her hand. "We're not done talking about the Jesse situation anyway."

Hali's smile fell.

"Yeah, you thought I forgot about that, didn't you?" Gray was amused despite himself. "When it's important for you, I'll never forget."

"You're kind of a pain," Hali complained.

"You love me anyway."

"Forever," she agreed.

Gray went soft all over. "Maybe I won't give you too hard of a time over it."

"Ah, something to look forward to."

2
TWO

Gray was careful when navigating Hali down the stairs to the beach once they were finished eating. Hali had—true to her word—eaten so much crab he was surprised she could walk at all. He took the dangerous steps on the incline, not bothering to ask if she was okay with it. Then, once they were close to the water, he put her down.

St. Pete Beach was not rocky. There was often a shattered shell line from the surf, but Hali had jokingly told him the soles of her feet were so tough she didn't feel the shells any longer. Gray was taking her at her word tonight.

She had to sit down to remove her sneakers. She couldn't walk in flip-flops yet, something that she was bitter about, and she couldn't balance enough on her healing hip to do it herself while standing. Once her shoes and socks were off, Gray kicked off his own and then pulled her to her feet again so they could walk in the surf.

They didn't go far—Hali's hip was healing but long distances were out of the question on sand—and after a few minutes, Hali plopped back down by her shoes and sighed.

"I miss the beach," she lamented.

Gray shot her a sidelong look. "You see the beach every day. I make sure of it."

"I knew you weren't itchy to drive the cart just for the heck of it," she said on a laugh. "It's not the same driving as it is walking." She lifted her nose. "It smells wonderful out here."

All Gray could smell with his super sensitive nose was the food from the restaurant. He opted not to ruin her good time, though. "Where do you want to live down the line?"

The question—the lack of finesse involved with it—threw Hali. "I ... don't know what you mean. I live in the villa."

"I know, and it's great for now. It's comfortable, and we're close to good food and water. One day, though, I'm imagining us with a kid or two. We can't live at the hotel."

"No. It might be kind of fun if we could, though. I mean...there are pools and miniature golf. There are pickleball courts and even a zip line. Our kids would never be bored." She rested her head against his shoulder. "Where do you want to live?"

Gray had been giving this a lot of thought. Not because they had to move anytime soon, but because they would have to save up for a house ... and location was everything in St. Pete.

"The only thing I know for sure is that I would prefer a house to a condo," he replied.

"I'm not saying I disagree, but why don't you want a condo?"

"Because I want a yard. Kids need a yard. I used to run

through the woods with Rusty for hours on end. Are you saying you didn't play outside?"

"No, I did. I still remember when my dad tried to teach me how to ride a bike. It didn't go well. I would want kids to have a soft landing when learning."

"Why didn't it go well?"

"Because my father is patient about most things, but riding a bike is not one of them. He got frustrated because I didn't seem to understand balance. I was ten before I learned how to ride a bike because I quit when he was trying to teach me, and eventually went back and taught myself."

Gray chuckled. "That sounds like something you would do."

"I like the idea of a house."

"We have time," he told her. "It's just something I would like to get a feel for so we can save up and look at neighborhoods."

"You're a planner," Hali noted. "I like that about you. In fact—" Whatever she was going to say died on her lips as the loud sound of a helicopter appeared out of nowhere. The blades were a whirring roar, and as the craft appeared overhead, she was momentarily blinded from the light it shined down on them. "What is that?" she demanded, shielding her eyes.

Gray was on his feet in an instant, his instincts kicking in. All around him, he could hear people exclaiming up and down the beach. His hearing was better than Hali's, which was part of his shifter genes, and the helicopter drowned everything else out for her.

It wasn't that way for him.

He could hear loud voices filing in from behind him, and when he looked, he realized that there were police officers flooding the beach. Not only that, but there were women in orange jumpsuits running in every direction ahead of the police officers.

He took stock of the situation in a split second.

"Prisoners," Hali said as she tried to get to her feet.

Gray grabbed her hand and hauled her up. "Prisoners, and the police are chasing them," he said. "I have to get you out of this mess."

He automatically reached for her, but Hali stopped him.

"We can help," she said.

Gray shook his head. "No. You'll get hurt."

Hali's eyes narrowed into dangerous slits. "I'm still the same person I always was. I might be slower, but I'm still Hali."

Gray looked pained. "Of course you are. They're prisoners, though."

"And I'm a witch."

He cocked his head. "Do you think you can do something under the radar to corral them?"

It was a question Hali didn't have an immediate answer to. "I can try."

"Then come on." Gray abandoned their shoes—they didn't have time to put them on, and sitting wasn't an option with all the activity—and slid his arm around her waist. "Don't argue with me," he ordered when she opened her mouth. "You're a miracle every single day of our lives together, but you can't run in the sand."

He was willing to do what was necessary to make her feel important and needed. He wasn't, however, willing to sit back and watch her injure her hip yet again. That was a bridge too far. He slid Hali into a spot between three palm trees—she would be relatively protected there—and then sent her an expectant look.

"Let's see what you've got," he prodded.

Hali knew she had to be careful. There were cops everywhere, although none of them seemed to be paying attention to the tourists. Or anybody not in an orange jumpsuit for that matter. To Hali, it would've been smarter to force the tourists out of the area. The entire flood of people—prisoners and police—seemed to have zero organization.

Hali licked her lips as she took in the prisoners. There were two trying to make their way into the water. "Are they going to try to swim away?" she asked.

"They're not thinking right now," Gray replied. "They're just trying to get away."

Hali unleashed a zippy spell she was quite fond of. It had both of the women pitching forward face first into the water. That allowed the police giving chase to catch them when they were on their knees. The women were hauled up in short order, cuffed, and then thrown onto the beach with a little more force than Hali was comfortable with.

"Well, that's not nice," she said. "That had to hurt."

Gray cast her a dubious look. "They're prisoners."

"They're still human beings." Hali turned back to the melee and tripped another fleeing prisoner so the pursuing police officer could grab her. "See." She gestured toward the duo. "He's much gentler."

"Geez." Gray rolled his eyes. "It's so you to get worked up over stuff like that." He grinned at her. "Do another one."

Hali didn't have to be convinced. Despite the fact that she was secured away between three trees, Gray serving as a wall of muscle to protect her, she was having fun. This was the most action she'd seen in weeks. Even when they'd taken down the merrow, she'd been removed from the action because of her hip. She'd been there but couldn't throw down with the others. It still made her itchy when she thought about it.

"There." She inclined her head toward two prisoners as they started for the stairs that led up to the patio where they'd just had their dinner. Her magic was fast and hot, and turned the stairs to fire fast enough that the prisoners screamed and fell backward. Within a split second, the stairs were back to normal, and the prisoners were on the ground.

"That was pretty impressive." Gray poked her side and leaned close, his lips next to her ear. "I'm kind of turned on, Hali."

Hali's mouth dropped open. "Are you flirting with me during a prison break? That's what this is, right?"

"I can't see an explanation for it other than that," he confirmed. "And, yes, I'm flirting with you. Do you have a problem with it?"

"Of course not. I was just checking."

Hali was feeling emboldened now. Sure, she hadn't done anything overly ambitious, but she also hadn't been hurt. She was in the thick of things, but not in any immediate danger. That was enough to have her footing—metaphorical and otherwise—solidify. She knocked down another two prisoners, allowed herself a moment to laugh, and then leaned into Gray.

He kissed the top of her head, seemingly thrilled that she was having a good time. She was so lost in the moment she almost didn't feel it. There was more magic there than her own, though, and it cascaded high enough she couldn't ignore it. The sensation of something dark crawling up her spine had her swiveling quickly, and she ran straight into Gray's chest.

"Move, handsome," she teased.

He was a wall of solid muscle, and he wasn't moving. Instead, he was staring into nothing, as if caught in a trance.

"Gray?" Alarm rippled over Hali as she waved her hand in front of his face. He didn't react. That's when she knew that something very bad had happened. "Gray?" She tried to touch him, but her hand was immediately repelled. Magic—much stronger than what she had been using—sparked and forced her back.

Gray didn't respond to her or the magic. He seemed to be focused on something outside of their little bubble. And whatever it was, it wasn't good.

When Gray started to move away from Hali, he looked to have a purpose. He stared straight through her and started toward the water, toward a police officer who had backed a blonde with dark roots in a jumpsuit against the water. Confused, Hali watched as Gray closed in on the duo. She was convinced he was about to wrestle the prisoner down ... right up until the moment when he took the officer by surprise, grabbed him by the back of the uniform shirt, and threw him in the water. Gray lifted the other man—who was smaller, but not dainty—as if he were a weight at the gym and then flung him several feet into the water as if he weighed nothing.

Hali's mouth fell open. "What in the hell?" she muttered. She took a step out of her safe haven and immediately regretted it. One of the prisoners—a younger woman who couldn't have been over the age of twenty—grabbed Hali by the arm.

"Give me your clothes," the prisoner ordered.

Hali made a face. "I'm going to have to decline."

"Give me your clothes!" the prisoner barked. She produced something sharp and lethal from her pocket—

Orange is the New Black had taught Hali it was called a shiv—and brandished it in front of Hali's face. "I'll gut you so fast you won't even see it coming," the woman threatened.

Hali opened her mouth, then shut it. Then she repeated the process. She had no idea what she was supposed to do here. "I'm going to have to decline," she repeated finally. "If you try to hurt me, you're going to regret it."

The prisoner unleashed an incredulous look. "Just who do you think you are?" She lashed out at Hali, aiming the shiv at her neck, but Hali had magic on her side and stripped the weapon from the woman at the same time she twisted the woman's hips. Since the prisoner's feet were planted and not moving, the hip swivel resulted in a cracking sound.

"Oh, gawd!" The prisoner fell to the sand and immediately reached for her ankle. "What did you do?"

The shiv had landed on the sand, and rather than being ignored, one of the other prisoners had picked it up. This woman was older, in her forties, and she had wild hair and eyes. "Give me your clothes!" she ordered Hali.

"What is it with you guys and my clothes?" Hali demanded. She glanced down at her blue shorts and gray top. "They're not expensive."

The new prisoner with the shiv made a face. "That's why we want them, honey. We stand out like sore thumbs in these jumpers."

"Oh." Hali nodded in understanding. "That makes sense. You can't have my clothes, though." She jerked up her chin and slammed the woman back, internally cringing when her body hit the ground, a shiver running through her thanks to the noise.

A police officer was on the fallen prisoner within a second. "Ma'am, get up to the restaurant," he ordered.

Hali glanced at him, weighed his order, and then kept moving toward Gray. He had intercepted another police officer and had him by the front of the shirt, his hand cocked back to deliver a punch. Before he could, Hali used her magic to drag the police officer from his grip. The officer's uniform ripped because Gray was holding on so tightly, but he was pulled across the sand a good twenty feet, and out of Gray's reach.

Gray's nostrils flared, but he didn't look up. He just stared into nothing, as if waiting for further instructions.

Slowly, Hali forced up her gaze. Behind Gray, a prisoner stood and stared Hali down. Unlike the other prisoners, she wasn't in a frenzy to escape. She was calm. Her light hair, although tangled from the wind, looked better kept than some of the other prisoners. Her face was devoid of makeup, but true beauty shone through.

She also looked evil.

"Interesting," the woman said as she regarded Hali. "You're a witch."

Hali nodded. She didn't know what to do. Gray was closer to the prisoner than her, and still out of it. She couldn't easily get to him. "You, too."

The other witch smiled. "We seem to be in a bit of a standoff here. Perhaps you should go."

"Not without him." Hali gestured toward Gray.

"Oh, is he yours?" The woman cocked her head. "He's quite the specimen. I can smell the shifter on him. I think it's best if you consider him a dead loss and move on, though. I'm going to be taking him with me."

"No, you're not." Hali would die before she let the other witch drag Gray off. It wasn't just that he would have no choice. She could do things to him, or rather force him to do things for her, that he would never get over. Hali couldn't let Gray leave this beach.

"Do you think you're stronger than me?" The other witch looked amused. "You're not. Trust me. The only way for you to survive this is to turn around and go."

"That's not happening." Hali countered. "I won't leave him."

"Fine." The other woman raised her head. "Kill her," she ordered Gray.

To Hali's horror, Gray took a step toward her. He didn't meet her gaze. He looked right through her. His steps weren't as fast as when he was heading toward the surf line to throw the police officer, though.

The witch's expression darkened when she realized Gray was dragging his feet. "Kill her!" she ordered, her fury evident.

Hali didn't know if Gray was strong enough to fight off the magic controlling him. She had no idea what magic was being used. She just knew that she had to stop Gray from hurting himself or others … so she did the only thing she could do. She knocked him down.

He hit the sand fairly hard and pitched forward. His hands clawed at the sand, but he couldn't find purchase. She'd made sure of that. Hali had essentially pinned him in place with her spell. He had no choice but to follow the other witch's orders. She'd taken the choice from him. Instead, she held him tight until he couldn't fight any longer and his face fell forward into the sand.

"That's cheating," the woman hissed.

"No, that's making sure that the right side wins," Hali countered. "He's down and out. You can't use him as a pawn. If you want out of this place, you have to go through me."

The witch laughed, but she didn't actually look amused. "I'm not afraid of you."

"You should be."

Before the witch could respond, a flare went up in the air. It was red, and bright, and illuminated the whole beach. Hali was momentarily distracted—as anybody would be—and looked up. Immediately, she caught herself and turned back so she wouldn't be vulnerable to an attack.

The spot where the other woman had been standing was empty. Hali scanned up and down the beach, determined to find her. She couldn't just let the woman escape. She was gone, though. Nowhere to be found.

On a sigh, Hali moved over to Gray. Her hip fought the extended effort it took to cross to him, but she ruthlessly shoved the pain out of her mind.

Gray's eyes were closed when she lowered herself to the sand next to him. The first thing she did was take his hand and press her fingers to his pulse point. She was relieved to find his heart beating normally. Then she put her hand to his forehead and pushed back his hair. His expression was peaceful enough, but she had no way of knowing who he would be when he woke up. Her spell had been enough to knock him out, but he wouldn't stay that way.

As women screamed around her, and police officers ordered everybody to lay down on the sand and put their hands behind their heads, Hali sat next to her boyfriend ... and hoped against hope that she hadn't somehow lost him.

The other witch had been powerful, and Hali wasn't expecting what happened, but she wasn't willing to lose Gray. One way or another, she would get him back.

They had a future to plan after all. That was a dream she would never let go of.

3
THREE

Gray was still out thirty minutes later when the scene was declared secure. Multiple officers had come up to try to take Gray from Hali, but she had staunchly refused and instead requested they call Detective Andrew Copeland. When they asked why, she just shook her head.

"I'm not going to move from this spot," she said in a clear voice. "He's not either. Obviously." She inclined her head toward Gray. "Just get Detective Copeland down here."

"And why would he come for some rando on the beach?" one of the uniformed offers demanded.

"Just tell him Hali Waverly is requesting his presence," she replied evenly. "He'll come."

And he did indeed come. Apparently, he'd been on the strip in front of the hotels when he got word that Hali was refusing to move. He made it to her side in five minutes from when she made the request, and he visibly blanched when he saw Gray unmoving on the sand.

"Is he...?" He couldn't finish the question.

Hali shook her head. "He's not dead. He's just out." She shot a sidelong look toward the officer who had positioned himself a mere ten feet away and then glanced back at Andrew.

He understood what she wasn't saying and moved up to the officer. "I've got this. I know Ms. Waverly and Mr. Hunter. You don't have to worry about him."

"He was in the water helping the escapees," the uniform shot back. "He's being arrested."

"Well, let me ascertain what we're dealing with," Andrew said. "We'll go from there." He waited until the uniform had taken off—a string of curses wafting through the air—and then he dropped down to his knees next to Gray. "What's going on here, Hali? Why do they think Gray was helping the prisoners?"

"Because he technically was." Hali kept her voice low as she filled him in. As the words poured out, Gray slowly began to stir. Her fingers were gentle as they traced over his skin, and part of her was dreading the moment when he would open his eyes and look at her.

What if it wasn't the man she loved staring back?

"So, let me get this straight." Andrew looked pained. "One of the prisoners—one you say you believe escaped—is magical and she somehow turned Gray into a zombie and that's why he threw a police officer in the Gulf. That's what you're saying, right?"

Hali nodded. "Pretty much. He wasn't a zombie, though. It was more like he was in a trance. She was issuing orders, he was following them, but he wasn't eating flesh or anything."

"Oh, well, at least we have that going for us." Andrew flicked his eyes to Gray as he slowly rocked to a sitting position. "Are you going to hurt me?"

Gray looked puzzled by the question. "I don't believe so, although...what am I doing here?"

"On the ground, or outside the restaurant?" Andrew asked.

"On the ground. We ate at the restaurant." Gray slid his eyes to Hali and found her blinking back tears. "Are you okay?" He instinctively reached for her and frowned when she put up a hand to stop him. "What happened?" He covered her hand with his. "What went down?"

Hali opened her mouth to respond, but Andrew silenced her with a headshake. "Let me take it from here, Hali," he warned. "It could be important."

Because Hali recognized that was true, she blew out a breath and remained silent.

"What do you remember?" Andrew queried. "And be specific."

"I..." Gray looked at Hali again. He didn't like the fear he saw reflected back. Whatever this was, it was important. He had to do as Andrew instructed. He trusted his childhood friend implicitly. "Um ... we went to dinner." Gray used the hand that wasn't wrapped around Hali's fingers to point at the balcony. "Hali had crab legs."

"I ate my weight in them," Hali said dully. She made an attempt at a smile, but it failed.

Gray wanted to reach for her again, but he knew better. Something was very wrong here.

"What did you have?" Andrew asked Gray.

Gray made a face. "Is that really important?"

"It could be if things come to a head. I want to set a baseline here. Just tell me."

"I had the surf and turf," Gray replied. "I had a big porterhouse with mushrooms and a lobster tail. Hali had all-you-can-eat crab legs. She had three plates."

Hali's mouth fell open. "I did not have three plates."

"You did so," Gray fired back. "I was keeping track."

"Well, they were small plates," Hali said to Andrew. "They were like salad plates, not dinner plates."

Andrew cracked a smile. "Thank you for the distinction."

"You're welcome."

"Any dessert?" Andrew asked.

Gray shook his head. "Hali likes key lime pie as much as the next person, but when she has a choice, she would rather stuff herself on crab than save room for pie."

"Ah, a girl after my own heart." Andrew winked at her. "What did you do after you ate?"

"We went for a walk on the beach," Gray replied. "Hali still has trouble with the sand. I helped take her shoes off."

"They're over there." Hali pointed toward a pile that was between the prone prisoners and the officers barking orders at them.

"I'll get them," Andrew promised.

"Good, because there's no way I can walk back to Paradise Lodge without shoes," Hali replied. "I won't make it. I'll probably have to stop fifty times to rest as it is."

"I'm carrying you," Gray countered. "Don't give me lip."

"You're not carrying her if you don't say the exact right things," Andrew countered. "You'll be in jail if this doesn't go the correct way."

Gray's mouth fell open. "Jail? What are you even talking about?"

"Lower your voice," Andrew warned. "I'm already out on a limb here."

"I don't understand," Gray gritted out. "What happened?"

"Just tell me what you remember," Andrew insisted. "It's important, Gray."

Gray read the tilt of his friend's head, the grim set to his jaw, and sighed. "We were on the beach talking about how we saw our future. I said I wanted us to buy a house instead of a condo. Hali admitted she didn't learn how to ride a bike until she was ten."

Andrew shot Hali an incredulous look. "What?"

"That's not as ridiculous as it sounds," Hali argued. "Lots of kids don't learn to ride bikes until later."

"Yes, most of the kids I know learn how to ride bikes when they're going into high school," Andrew said dryly. "That's totally true."

Hali murdered him with a look. "Not high school. I was still in elementary school ... for another year." She turned morose. "I was drawing a line in the sand with my father because he was overbearing when it came to teaching us how to ride bikes."

"If that's your story." Andrew was blasé as he met Gray's gaze. "Finish it out."

"We were having a good time and then ... and then..." His eyes moved to Hali and clouded over, causing her heart to skip a beat.

"Stay with me," she ordered, grabbing the front of his shirt. "Don't leave me again."

When Gray's vision cleared, he looked frustrated. "I can't remember what happened after. I think there were people on the beach. Everything gets really hazy, though."

Andrew nodded before flicking his eyes to Hali. "I'm going to leave it to you to explain what happened to him. I don't suppose you can give him a magical bump on the head so I can get the two of you out of here, though, can you?"

Hali's eyes widened. "You want me to hit him?"

"No, I want you to make it so it looks as if someone else did."

Realization dawned on Hali. "Oh, right. I can do that."

"Can you do it with people watching? I'm going to touch the back of his head and act like I found something. I want you to touch it when I tell you, like I'm asking you to confirm. The story is that one of the prisoners struck him over the head when they flooded the beach. Are you following?"

Hali nodded. "I've got it."

Andrew reached for Gray's head. "Don't be weird about this," he ordered his friend. "If this doesn't go as planned, you will be sitting in a jail cell in twenty minutes."

Gray was confused but did as instructed. When Hali touched him, he felt something warm pulse through him. Then an actual ache became apparent on the back of his head.

"There's definitely a bump," Andrew offered, his voice carrying. "You need to take him to see a doctor, Hali. Isn't there one on staff down at Paradise Lodge?"

"There is," Hali confirmed. "I'll arrange a ride because I can't drive. I can call one of the bellhops down to drive Gray's truck back."

"You can't drive?" Now Andrew was the one who looked confused.

"I can't drive his truck," Hali clarified. "It's too far of a stretch for my leg because of my hip."

"Ah. Okay." Andrew squeezed her shoulder. "Gray can't drive with that blow to his head. Get someone to look at him at the resort." He lowered his voice. "Get documentation however you need to get it. Concussion." That was all he said.

Hali's smile was tight. "Come on, baby." She tugged on Gray's arm. "It will be okay."

Andrew scooped up their discarded shoes and handed them to Gray. "Do what Hali tells you to do."

Gray was still confused. He'd managed to put some of it together, though. "Why were there prisoners on the beach?" he asked as he held the shoes against his chest.

"Prison bus accident, just out on the main road," Andrew replied. "It tilted on its side, and they all fled. We're not sure how it happened yet. I can guarantee I'll be in touch, though."

"Okay." Gray allowed Hali to slowly lead him up the beach. He wanted to pick her up, but for some reason he didn't dare touch her. Something had happened when he was out of it. He didn't know what, but he wasn't an idiot. It had been bad.

He was furious about whatever it was because the way she'd pulled back when he'd reached for her was seared into his memory. Someone had done something, and he would make them pay for wedging a single ounce of mistrust into their relationship.

"I'm sure I'll see you tomorrow then," Gray said.

Andrew bobbed his head. "Count on it."

HALI HAD NO TROUBLE GETTING SOMEONE DOWN to the restaurant to drive Gray's truck. He sat in the back because it was hard for her to crawl into the limited space with her hip. Once back at the resort, the bellhop parked in front of the villa. He promised to send the doctor over as soon as he could.

Hali smiled because it was expected, but weariness threatened to take her over as she crawled out of the truck.

She had to go legs first because she couldn't risk a jump. She held on to the seat to give herself balance. When she straightened, she found Gray was already out of the truck and staring at her.

"Did I hurt you?" He looked horrified at the thought.

"No," she assured him. She grabbed his hand. "Inside. We'll talk about it inside."

Gray remained rooted to his spot. "You're acting as if I hurt you. I would never purposely do that." He blinked back tears he didn't even realize he was close to shedding. "Do you want me to go?"

Hali did the world's biggest double take. "Of course not. This just isn't something we should be talking about in the open." She wrapped her fingers around his arm and pulled. She hadn't put her shoes back on in the truck, so she was barefoot. The cement was still warm under her feet from a full day of baking in the sun. "Nobody is going anywhere."

Gray let her lead him to the stairs. When he reached for her so he could carry her up them—they were being especially careful with stairs right now—she didn't nudge him back. He took that as a good sign, even as a storm raged inside of him.

"Sit down," Hali instructed, once they were inside, gesturing toward the couch. "I'm closing the blinds. I very much doubt the witch is anywhere near this place—she's probably long gone by now—but it's better to be safe than sorry."

"What witch?" Gray demanded.

"Shh." Hali pressed a kiss to his forehead as he sat on the couch. "Two minutes."

She double-checked all the windows and blinds and then returned to the living room. Gray was in exactly the same spot, and he looked close to a meltdown.

"Okay." She took his hand as she sat down next to him. "Here it is."

He wouldn't want it sugarcoated, so she didn't bother wasting time. She told him everything. When she got to the part of the story where he was heading for her and she had no choice but to magically knock him down and out, she cringed and waited for the explosion.

"I'm so sorry," she said. "I didn't want to hurt you. I didn't know what else to do though. Please don't be mad."

All of the oxygen Gray had been holding inside whooshed out, and he crushed her against his chest, burying his face in her hair.

"I really am sorry," she continued. "I just didn't have enough time to think. I didn't know what else to do."

"Baby, don't," he said in a husky voice. "You did the exact right thing."

She jerked up her chin, hope flooding her features. "You're not angry with me?"

"No, Hali, I'm not angry with you." He traced his fingers over her cheek. "I'm the one who is sorry. I don't remember any of that. It's as if I was out there on the beach with you, then everything blurs. Like … it's as if things were on fast forward on an old VHS tape. Things went so fast they became blurry. Then they slowed down again."

He rested his forehead against hers. "I didn't hurt you, right? Tell me if I did. I don't know what I'll do to fix it, but I have to know."

"You didn't hurt me," she assured him. "You didn't even get close enough to hurt me. You did, however, throw a police officer a good fifteen feet into the surf. I really hope the cameras are too grainy for them to make that out. You were also about to pound another police officer, but I used my magic and kind of spirited him away."

"You did the right thing," he repeated. He leaned back against the couch and pulled her with him. "You did the exact right thing." He ran his hands over her back, his mind wandering to the fear she must have felt when she realized the man she loved was coming at her with the intent to harm her. He wanted to believe he would've somehow shaken himself out of it before it got that far, but he couldn't cross that bridge.

"Listen to me." He stroked his hand over her hair as he pushed her back far enough to see her face. He kept his hands cupping the back of her head. "I don't know what happened out there. I don't know why it happened either. All I know is that I love you and I'm so sorry. You were the hero tonight. Don't ever doubt that."

Hali sucked in a sniffle. "You don't have to be sorry. It's not as if you were in control of what happened. That witch made you do it."

"I don't care. It shouldn't have happened. You shouldn't even let me touch you right now."

"Oh, let's not make it weird," she countered. "I want you to touch me."

He gripped her tighter. "I'm so sorry."

"Stop apologizing," Hali ordered. "You didn't do this. You were forced to do it. By the way, you're going to have to pretend you have a concussion. We can force the resort doctor to say whatever we want—Franklin owes me, so he'll make sure of it—but you have to pretend it's true. They'll throw you in jail otherwise."

"Maybe I belong in jail," he countered. "Maybe that's what I deserve."

"I told you not to be weird." Hali was fierce when she pulled back. "I get that you feel guilty—part of me even understands why—but you're not to blame here. We need to work together to figure out who that witch even is."

"Why? Why do we care who she is?"

"Because she saw me using my magic, and she wanted to take you with her. I don't think she likes that I outsmarted her."

"You are my little genius." He pressed a kiss to her forehead.

She smiled, happy to see that he was coming out of his funk. "I don't believe she's done with us. Plus, I don't think she was the only prisoner who escaped. Just because some of them ran down to the beach like morons, that doesn't mean all of them did. She's out there, and I'm betting a few of the others are too."

"Do you think she'll come after you?" Gray asked. He hated the idea. "Maybe ... maybe I shouldn't be here with you in case she does come back. Although, I don't like the thought of being away from you. You might be safer if I'm gone, though."

"Nobody is going anywhere." Hali was firm. "I want you here." In truth, she needed him with her. She'd come to rely on him, and for so much more than just the occasional lift because she couldn't walk somewhere. "We're going to figure this out together. I need you not to sit around feeling sorry for yourself, though. That's not going to get us anywhere."

"I just won't be able to bear it if I hurt you."

"I understand that. I feel the same way about you, which is why we keep going around about your mother. Nobody is going to hurt anybody, though. We're going to be okay. We were caught unaware the first time. That won't happen again."

"Is there something you can do to ensure that I can't be overtaken again?" He looked hopeful.

Hali didn't want to crush that hope, but she couldn't lie to him. "I don't know. Not that I'm aware of. I'll call my grandmother first thing in the morning, though. She's the most powerful witch I know. She should be able to figure it out."

Gray sighed again. "Okay, but we need to be proactive. If I were to hurt you..." He couldn't finish.

"You're not going to hurt me. Have faith." She took his hand and squeezed. "We've got a happily ever after in our future. I guarantee it."

Gray needed to believe it, so he did. "Okay. I just want to do this until the doctor gets here and gives us my fake diagnosis. That was smart thinking on Andrew's part, by the way."

"It was," Hali agreed. "I'm not sure we're out of the worst of it just yet, though."

Gray didn't want to think about that. "Just sit here and let me love you. We'll figure out the rest in the morning, huh? I just need to close my eyes."

Hali let him. His heart was troubled. He needed to get over that before he could help her ... and she *would* need his help. One way or another.

4
FOUR

Gray woke before Hali the next morning and was careful not to shift too much. He wanted her to get as much sleep as possible. Reclaiming her tiki bar today, while exciting for her, would leave her feeling exhausted by the end of her shift. He would've preferred she start out light, with half of a shift, but he didn't get a say in the matter.

Plus, if she went much longer without being able to run her bar how she wanted to run it, she would explode. An angry Hali was a loud Hali.

It wasn't just Hali taking over the tiki bar that was bothering him, though. He was worried about the previous night. Hali had gone out of her way to tell him that he hadn't hurt her, and she wasn't afraid, but he still remembered all too well the way she hadn't automatically gone to him when he'd reached for her after the event. They were always so in tune, always so aware of each other. Most of the time she was already reaching for him when he was reaching for her. He did not want this incident creating a wedge in their relationship. That would kill him.

On a sigh, Hali shifted and snuggled in closer to him. She was still out, but Gray knew she would be waking up soon. He often watched her first thing in the morning. He liked how cuddly she was, how unguarded she was in sleep. Now when he looked down at her, she seemed vulnerable. He didn't like it.

Perhaps sensing that he was awake and watching her, Hali shifted again and opened her eyes. They immediately lasered on Gray. "Are you going to be weird today?" she asked in a soft voice that was still raspy from sleep.

"I'm going to try not to be," he replied as he stroked his hand over her hair. It was snarled from heavy sleep, but he didn't care. One of the first things he noticed about her was how breathtaking she was. The second thing he noticed was her mouth. He liked a fiery woman, and Hali had that in spades. She was everything he never knew he wanted, and he was desperate not to lose her.

Being a danger to her was also not an option.

"We should check in with Andrew," he said. "I have my doctor's note that I have a concussion. We should probably get that to him."

"Yeah." Hali slid her hand over his chest. "Are you still being a baby over what happened last night?"

"I'm not being a baby," he protested. "I just don't like it."

"Well, I don't like it either. Nobody was seriously hurt, though."

"You could've been hurt."

"I would've protected myself no matter what," she argued. "I would've protected you, too."

"You *did* protect me," he confirmed. "Knocking me out was the smartest thing you could've done."

"But I hurt you in the process. How come you're not angry about that?"

"See, I can see what you're doing." He stared hard into her eyes. "Don't. You only knocked me down because I was coming at you. You did the exact right thing."

"So you told me last night. I was just making sure." She poked his side and elicited a grin. "Just for the record, despite the fact that she had control—which is an invasion that needs to be talked about at some point—you were showing signs of fighting her. You were walking really slowly and didn't just hop to her order. I think you were fighting it, and she didn't like it."

That was some measure of relief to Gray, although not as much as he needed to put the incident behind him. "I guess that's something. I still want an update from Andrew."

"Maybe he can meet us for breakfast."

Gray nodded. "That's a good idea. Are you hungry?"

Her stomach let loose a ruthless growl on cue. "What do you think?" she asked on a giggle.

"I think I need to feed you, and then we'll start figuring things out. It does me no good to wallow."

"I believe that's what I was telling you last night."

"You were, but I wasn't ready to listen."

"And now?" Hali was genuinely curious.

"And now I want to make sure it never happens again. I won't hurt you. I just ... won't."

Hali rested her head on his chest, her ear over his heart. "I know. I'm not struggling like you are. I know, though."

Gray hoped that was true.

. . .

HE TEXTED ANDREW TO MEET THEM FOR breakfast, and then they took hasty showers. Because Hali was returning to work, she needed comfortable shorts. She went with a pair of sky-blue drawstring shorts that she never would've considered wearing to work two months before. She needed something that would be easy to get on and off during bathroom breaks, though. She paired the shorts with a white polo shirt and had Gray help her pull her hair back in a neat ponytail. It was still wet and would dry funny, but it was easier to have out of her way.

"How do I look?" she asked as she appeared in the doorway that separated the hallway from the living room.

Gray looked up from his phone screen and grinned. "You look like a good girl who is about to take the world by storm."

Hali rolled her eyes. "I'm not a good girl. I'm a bad girl with a dream."

"If you say so."

Hali was having none of it. "I know so." She inclined her head toward the door. "Let's go. I'm starving."

"Um ... aren't you forgetting something?" Gray gestured toward her bare feet.

"My shoes are in your truck. I didn't bother with them last night." She whipped a pair of fresh socks out of her pocket. "I figured we could pick them up on the way to breakfast."

"Good idea." Gray double-checked that the door had latched when they were leaving. It didn't always happen because of the keycard reader, and he wanted to make sure. Once he was, he took her hand and started across the parking lot. Her shoes were on the passenger side, so he lifted her up to the seat and took the socks from her.

"You don't have to do that," Hali protested.

"I like to." He gave her a quick kiss. "Pretty soon, you're not going to need me for anything. I'm going to miss being the guy you relied on to help you with almost everything."

"Oh, I'm still going to need you," Hali assured him as he pulled on one of the socks. "Who else is going to buy me crab legs?"

He chuckled. "Good point."

Once her shoes and socks were on, he helped her hop down. Then he took her hand again. She was getting good at walking on the sidewalks. She still faltered around slippery surfaces and took her time when there was an incline, but it had only been a few weeks. She was working hard to get back to full autonomy. It made him sort of sad.

"I don't suppose you would be willing to let me carry you home from work every now and again would you?" he asked out of the blue.

Hali shot him a sidelong look. "Why?"

"Because I like carrying you. We can turn it into a private game."

"If you have some weird princess fetish that I don't know about, keep it that way."

"I was thinking more along the lines of that old movie *An Officer And a Gentleman*, but sure."

Hali's forehead pinched in concentration. "I think my grandmother used to watch that movie."

"My mother loves it," Gray said. "I kind of want to create a specific game so I can still get my jollies."

Hali laughed, as he'd intended. "I'll think about it."

"Thank you." He gave her hand a lavish kiss. "You're too good to me."

They were still laughing when they arrived at the restaurant. Mindy Grant was standing near the door when they walked in. She was Hali's favorite server at the restaurant, and she was always up on the gossip. Mindy wasn't smiling today, though.

"Your breakfast guest is here." She pointed toward Andrew, who was already at a table and drinking coffee. "He seems like he's in a foul mood, which is too bad, because I find him hot."

"Do you want me to see if he's open to a setup?" Hali asked.

"I don't know. Is he always going to be that pouty?" Mindy looked torn. "I mean ... he's been in here before, and he has a nice smile. He doesn't look as if he's going to be using that smile anytime soon."

Hali followed her friend's gaze. "He's got a lot on his mind. Let me feel him out, huh? He might not be open for suggestions until after his current case is closed."

"Would that be all the prisoners who escaped last night?" Mindy asked.

Hali nodded. "Did you see a news update on that? How many of them are still missing?"

"Last I heard was ten. They didn't have a firm number, though. How do you not know how many prisoners are missing?"

"Well, the bus turned over," Gray replied. "Some of the prisoners were likely injured in the initial accident and transported to the hospital. Some of the deputies would've been in there with them. Then some of the prisoners didn't flee and remained by the bus. Then you have the ones that did flee. You have to get all those prisoners to the same place to count them off. Given the ones in the hospital—and the ones who might've been picked up by local law enforcement rather than county down the road—I can see why they don't have a firm number yet."

Mindy blinked. "Huh. When you put it like that. Definitely feel him out. I guess he has a right to be depressed right now."

"I'm on it." Hali squeezed her friend's wrist and started for the table.

Andrew hopped up when he saw Hali. He reached for a chair to pull it out for her, but Gray beat him to it.

"How are things?" Hali asked as she sat down. Her smile was wide as she shifted on the chair and glanced up at Gray. "My hip doesn't hurt at all." She shouldn't have been so excited about making a five-minute walk without pain, but she was.

And that broke Gray's heart a little bit, because how much pain was she in every single day that she was so excited about this? She'd normalized the pain, and he didn't like it. "I'm glad, baby."

"Aw, so cute," Andrew drawled as he watched them stare into each other's eyes for several seconds. "Just so stinking cute."

Gray made a face as he turned back to his friend. "Sorry. She's just so pretty I can't look away from her."

"Speaking of pretty, my friend Mindy is interested if you pull that stick out of your butt," Hali said sweetly.

Andrew glanced over his shoulder at the server, seemed to consider it a moment, then sighed. "I have to get through this first." He was all business as he turned back to Hali and Gray. "I am interested, but it's going to be weeks at this point before I can even pretend to go out on a date."

"That bad, huh?" Gray's worry kicked up a notch. "Tell us what you've got."

"First off, tell me you got the doctor's report I asked for," Andrew prodded.

"Yup." Hali pulled out a Paradise Lodge folder. The note was inside. "We got it last night and have ensured that Gray will be under our illustrious doctor's care for at least a week."

"Good." Andrew scanned the letter and nodded. "Right now, all they have is Gray walking into the surf. You can't even see him fighting with another officer. That officer is confused, but swears he remembers Gray coming at him. My plan is to argue that Gray was confused by the blow he took to his head."

Hali darted a look toward Gray. "He won't go to jail, will he? I can't bear the thought of that."

"He won't go to jail," Andrew promised. "There might be some hard questions coming—by someone other than me—but as long as Gray sticks to the script and says he doesn't remember any of it, it will be fine."

"I *don't* remember any of it," Gray said. "It's a blur, and I don't like that. I could've hurt Hali."

"You didn't, though," Andrew said. "I get being upset—completely and totally—but you can't crawl into a hole of self-loathing and live there. I'm probably going to need you guys."

Gray perked up. "Whatever you need. I want to end this."

"Well, I'm probably going to be coming by later with a list and photos of all the prisoners who are still missing," Andrew said. "I want to see if you recognize any of them."

"One of them has to be the witch who hexed Gray," Hali insisted. "She disappeared right before the rest of the prisoners were taken down."

"My guess is that she'll be among the missing," Andrew confirmed. "I should have that list within a few hours."

Mindy picked that moment to come to their table with her pad. "Are you guys ready to order?" she asked sweetly. Her smile—and cleavage—was pointed directly at Andrew.

"Um … I'll have some pancakes," Andrew said. "That's okay, right?" Suddenly, he looked flustered.

Gray shot Hali an amused look. "I'll have the blueberry pancakes, too," he said. "Please add a side of bacon to it."

"Ooh. I'll have bacon, too." Andrew's cheeks flushed with a bit of color as he handed his menu back to Mindy. "Thank you."

"You're welcome." Mindy was clearly pleased because her smile was on full display when she turned to Hali. "What about you?"

"I want eggs, corned beef hash, and toast," Hali replied. "I also want a side of sausage and a cup of fresh fruit." She handed Mindy her menu. "I also want a big glass of tomato juice and some coffee."

Mindy arched an eyebrow. "Somebody is hungry."

"I'm getting my bar back today." Hali rubbed her hands together, reminding Gray of a kid on Christmas morning. "I need my strength."

"Aw, I didn't realize you were going back to work so soon. I thought the big guy here would keep you in bed for another few weeks." She lightly slapped Gray's shoulder.

"That was my plan," Gray confirmed. "She can't be controlled, though."

"Not even a little," Hali agreed. She was all smiles. "I'm really excited."

"Then I'll make sure they give you extra food," Mindy promised. "I'll be right back with your drinks."

Andrew watched her go, his gaze intense. When he turned back and found Hali and Gray watching him with unveiled interest, he was sheepish. "Sorry. What were we talking about?"

"How you have a crush on Mindy," Gray replied. "And how adorable it is."

"Don't push it." Andrew jabbed a finger in his direction and then went back to being serious. "So, we believe as many as ten inmates are still out there. Most of them are likely going to be in this immediate area, because getting someone to stop when you're wearing an orange prison jumpsuit can't be easy."

"They know that, though," Hali argued. "Two of them tried to attack me with shivs on the beach last night. Both of them wanted my clothes."

Gray shuddered. "You didn't mention that."

"Because it wasn't important. I knocked them both down easily and they were taken into custody."

"I'm going to want to know who threatened you with a weapon," Andrew said. "That will merit extra charges. Do you think you can remember their faces?"

Hali nodded. "Sure. They didn't get near me, though."

"They still threatened you. It's going to take weeks to sort out the various extra charges we have coming in. It's a mess." Andrew exhaled heavily and rolled his neck. "As for the one who took Gray over, she's going to be a concern for another reason."

Hali had already figured that out herself. "If she can take over Gray, that means she can take over others. She's going to be your biggest concern."

"Yes, and I can't tell very many people why she's going to be my biggest concern," Andrew said. "Not everybody—or even most everybody—is aware of the paranormal world. It's going to turn into a mess."

"If this prisoner has magic at her disposal, why was she behind bars in the first place?" Gray asked. "Why didn't she use her magic to escape before now?"

Andrew held out his hands. "I can't answer that. I just don't know. Right now, the most important thing is to identify her. We need the identities because most of these women are going to have no choice but to return to friends and family for help. It's not as if they knew they were getting out."

"Will most of them get caught right away because they're not prepared?" Hali asked.

"Most of them," Andrew confirmed. "It's the ones who aren't caught in the first forty-eight hours who are going to be trouble. The longer they're out, the safer they'll feel."

"What about the really desperate ones?" Gray asked. "Won't they be a danger to the general populace? There have to be some prisoners in there who realize they made a mistake when running and that capture is inevitable. Won't they do something stupid to make sure that doesn't happen?"

"In theory," Andrew confirmed. "We're going to put it out there in about an hour that anybody who turns herself in will not be facing extra charges. We want to use it as an enticement."

Hali straightened in her chair. "Will that work?"

"On one or two," Andrew replied. "The community is still going to be in danger, though. The fact that one of them is magical—and can force people to fight for her—is another problem. We could lose a lot of lives before this is all said and done."

"What do you want us to do?" Hali asked. "Like ... do you want me to go looking for this witch? I'll be able to recognize her."

"No." Andrew was firm when he shook his head. "You're not at a hundred percent."

Hali balked. "I'm fine."

"Stop." Andrew held up his hand. "I get that you want to stand on your own two feet and don't like being treated as breakable. I really do get it. You're not a hundred percent, though, and I'm afraid of what could happen with this other witch if she manages to gain control of you."

It was something Hali hadn't considered. "I'm not afraid of her," she said finally. "I can help you."

"For now, the biggest worry is identifying who we're dealing with. After that, I'll let you know."

Because she had no choice, Hali nodded. "Okay. You're in charge. We'll just follow your lead."

"Well, since I don't know what I'm doing, that should be fun." Andrew cracked a smile. "Now tell me about your friend." He lowered his voice to a conspiratorial whisper. "I want to know everything about her."

Hali grinned. "I'm glad you asked. I think you two might be good together."

"You let me be the judge of that, Miss Busybody."

"Yeah, yeah, yeah."

5
FIVE

Hali's mind was on multiple things when they left the restaurant. She had her bar back, and she couldn't wait to be in charge again. On the flip side, Andrew's worry had been palpable. There was something he wasn't saying.

"What do you think?" she asked Gray once they'd said goodbye to the detective and were on their way to the tiki bar. It was a short walk, but Hali wanted to open the hut early so she could reclaim her territory.

"I think that Andrew is worried about something specific, and he hasn't told us what it is yet," Gray replied.

Hali was relieved they were on the same page. "What could he be keeping?"

"I don't know. I..." Gray trailed off.

Hali immediately jerked up her chin. If the witch was back, she would protect Gray before she got her hooks into him this time. She would get ahead of the problem and make sure Gray wasn't victimized twice. To her utter surprise, though, it wasn't the witch waiting for them at the tiki bar. No, that honor went to Harlan and Helene

Hunter, Gray's parents. They were sitting in the shadows on the patio and seemed to be having an intense conversation.

"Uh-oh." Hali shot Gray a worried sidelong look. "Maybe if you run now, they won't catch you."

Gray made a face. "I'm not leaving you, and I know nothing is dragging you away from this bar until you check each and every bottle of liquor and garnish tray yourself."

"You could come back later. I'll be fine. Nobody will be out here for a few hours."

The look he shot her was withering. "What part of 'I'm not leaving you' don't you understand?"

"Your mood is lovely," Hali commented. Unlike her boyfriend, she planted a bright smile on her face as she approached the Hunters. "This is a nice surprise. Let me open up and get everything going, and then I'll make you some drinks."

"Oh, we don't need drinks," Helene said hurriedly.

"Speak for yourself," Harlan countered. "I want a drink. I told you this was a bad idea—pushing him is *always* a bad idea—but you refuse to listen. That means I want a drink."

Helene made an exasperated sighing sound. "Why do you always have to be so difficult?" she complained.

"That's simply what I do." Harlan flashed a smile for Hali's benefit. "How is your hip?"

"Better," Hali replied. She grunted as she tried to lift the sliding cage that covered the tiki bar window during off hours. Normally, it wasn't an issue, but she usually put weight on her hip when doing it.

Calmly, Gray moved in behind her and tugged up the cage with little effort. "Seems you do need me after all," he said in a low voice.

Hali pursed her lips. "I would kiss you as a reward, but it feels weird with your parents here."

He lightly patted her bottom. "Go inside and rest."

Hali's eyebrows pulled together. "Um ... I'm just getting started. How about you go and sit with your parents, and you take a rest?" she challenged.

Gray made a guttural sound in his throat but headed in that direction anyway. It was the last thing he wanted, but he knew causing a scene now would just make Hali anxious. After what had happened the previous evening, he didn't want that.

"Father," he said as he sat down next to Harlan. He didn't acknowledge his mother.

"Let's not make this more difficult than it has to be, huh?" Harlan suggested. "Your mother and I are here because we want you to know that we've managed to put together some leads on Russell."

Gray frowned. Russell Greason had fled in the wake of the merrow loss. He'd been working with them and knew he wouldn't survive if he was found during the battle. He might've been the current pack leader, but everybody was looking for him. He either had to die or cede the pack leadership. Right now, he was in the wind.

"You made a list?" Gray kept his expression bland. "I'll take it. Rusty and I have been talking about heading out and taking a look."

"You can do that today," Hali suggested from the inside of the tiki hut. "Oh, who moved the cherries in the refrigerator? I had them exactly where I wanted them."

Even though he wasn't keen to spend time with his parents, Gray couldn't help but smile at her beleaguered tone.

"She looks good," Harlan noted. "Is she feeling okay?"

Gray wasn't nearly as angry with his father as he was his mother. His father, while emotionally distant at times, had been making an effort. He also had no idea that his wife was actively trying to get Hali killed. Gray appreciated that.

That didn't mean he was in the mood for a heart-to-heart. "She's good," Gray replied. "She's going to need to rest later, no matter what she believes."

"I heard that," Hali barked. "You let me worry about resting. You have a crazy pack leader to find."

Gray smirked again, love welling up inside of him. "I'm waiting until Jesse gets here so she's not alone. I'm leaving him with firm instructions to make her sit down at least fifteen minutes every hour."

"What's her doctor say?" Helene asked.

Gray pretended he hadn't heard her. "I'll take the list," he said to his father. "My initial plan wasn't to leave the tiki bar today, but I have a feeling if I don't, there's going to be a fight." He cast a fond look toward Hali as she threw a rag across the inside of the hut.

"They moved everything," she exclaimed. "Nothing is where I left it. I'm going to kill both of them."

Harlan watched his son, caught between amusement and sadness. Gray looked at Hali the same way he looked at Helene. Of course, Hali hadn't been accused of working with the enemy ... at least as far as he could tell. "Son," he started.

Gray held up his hand to hold off whatever his father was going to say.

"I'm going to kill Rusty," Hali announced as she appeared in the window. "He switched it out so the tequilas are at the back and the vodka is at the front. Everybody knows you use the tequila more than the vodka at a tiki bar."

Gray grinned. "I'll tell him he's on your list the second I see him."

"Tell him there's going to be pain." Hali shook her fist before disappearing from view again.

"Do you know what you're going to do with Russell when you find him?" Harlan asked.

"Well, killing him seems like the best option I have," Gray replied. "He did try to kill my girlfriend. I think he has it coming."

"I don't disagree," Harlan assured him. "He *does* have it coming. The thing is, if you kill him away from the others, there will always be questions."

"Questions about what?" Gray demanded.

"Well, if you're going to step into a leadership role—"

Gray cut off Harlan before he could finish it out. "I have no interest in being in a leadership role in the pack."

"But you're the person everybody wants to be in control," Helene countered. She didn't shy away from Gray's glare. "Be as mad as you want at me," she said. "I've earned it. I get it. The pack is relying on you, though."

"I'm not going to be the leader," Gray insisted. "Heck, I'm not going to be a member of the pack at all. That's not why I'm going after Russell."

"So, why are you going after Russell?" Harlan asked. "He's no longer a threat. If you don't care about the pack, why do you care about him?"

"Because he's a threat to Hali," Gray replied. "I'm not just going to let him sit in a cabin somewhere and stew. He'll come back angry, under the cover of darkness, and try to hurt her. There's no way I will allow that to happen."

Harlan looked dubious. "If you would just consider it—"

Gray cut him off with a firm headshake. "I'm not considering it. That's not the life I want. Hali and I want a house, with a yard so kids can play, and a driveway so we can teach them how to ride their bikes. Well, maybe not Hali. It turns out she didn't learn to ride a bike until she was ten, so she might not have a lot to offer in that department."

"I heard that," Hali barked from inside the tiki hut. Gray couldn't see her face, but he could picture it, so he smiled. "Keep it up and you really will be sleeping on the couch tonight."

Gray wasn't overly worried. "Russell is a threat to the person I love the most. He's also a threat to Rusty, who very well could be the new pack leader. He doesn't get a free ride. That doesn't mean I want to take his place, though."

Harlan heaved out a sigh before sliding a sheet of paper toward Gray. "You've always had a head like a brick."

"I have," Gray agreed. "That's not going to change. I know what I want. A leadership position in the pack isn't in there."

"Then good luck finding Russell," Harlan said. "He's going to have a few people surrounding him who are still loyal. It won't be many, though. The writing is on the wall. People are not going to stick with him."

"That's good, because he's going down."

"Good luck."

Gray was grim. "Thanks. I think I'm going to need it."

"FUN FACT, THE EIFFEL TOWER GETS TALLER in hot weather."

Hali paused by the open window, fixed her regular customer Lana Silver with a flat look, and debated if she wanted to take the ultimate plunge. She decided she had no choice. "How?" she demanded.

"Oh, I know the answer to this." Jesse bumped his sister

out of the way, paying no mind to her recovering hip, and planted himself in front of Lana. He had a look of absolute adoration on his face. "It's because when iron heats up, it expands."

Lana nodded happily. "Yes. It's called thermal expansion, and the Eiffel Tower can be as much as six inches taller."

"Wow," Hali said as Jesse and Lana high-fived. She'd always known her brother was a bit of a geek, but she'd never pictured him with Lana. At this point, she had no idea how far their relationship had gone. They seemed to be having a grand time together, though. "You learn something new every day, huh?"

Lana nodded happily. "I'll have another one." She pushed her empty glass toward Jesse, who happily accepted it.

Hali turned away from the two of them and focused on Annabelle Hutchinson, who often brought her laptop to the tiki bar so she could drink while working. "Aren't you thrilled with that little tidbit?" she asked the attorney.

Annabelle shrugged, catching Hali off guard. "It's better than a lot of the other fun facts she's come up with."

"True story," Hali mused. "How about you?" She motioned toward Annabelle's half-melted drink. "Are you good?"

"For now," Annabelle replied. She sipped her drink before continuing. "How are you feeling? I noticed you cringe there for a second when your brother ran into you. He didn't hurt you, did he?"

Jesse, who was just behind his sister, froze. "I didn't mean to do that," he said after a few seconds. "Don't tell Dad I did that. Don't tell Grandma ... or Mom for that matter either. They'll give me grief."

Hali patted her brother's shoulder. "It's fine," she assured him. "I thought it was going to hurt, but it didn't. I've been doing that a lot lately."

"Assuming things will hurt because they used to?" Annabelle queried. Her gaze was sympathetic. "I can see that. I bet things will get better when you're more used to the free range of movement, though."

"Probably," Hali agreed. "I feel a lot better than I did. I still can't walk freely on the beach, though."

"Did the doctor say you should be walking freely on the beach at this point?"

Hali shook her head. "I'm not even supposed to try for another few weeks. We were out there last night when the prisoners arrived, though, so I got a little preview. It wasn't terrible."

"You were out there for that?" Lana's eyes went wide. "I was so glad I left the tiki bar early last night when I heard what happened."

"It didn't happen here," Hali countered.

"No, but what was to stop them from running down here?" Lana challenged. "They could've come down here and killed us all."

"They seemed a lot more interested in running," Hali replied. "Two of them tried to get me to give them my clothes."

"It makes sense," Annabelle remarked after taking another sip of her cocktail. "They can't hide in those jumpers. That's by design. Their only shot of getting away would be to find a change of clothes so they can melt in with the locals."

"Some of them got away, though," Hali said. "We're waiting to see a final list." She didn't mention the witchy shenanigans that had overtaken Gray. It wasn't a story she wanted to spread. "They think as many as ten of them are still out there."

"That's freaky when you think about it," Jesse said. "How do we know that one of them didn't hide in the bushes here, attack a tourist, take her room card and is right now pretending to be a guest here?" He gestured toward the tables, which were half full. It was early in the day, so the heat was oppressive. The bar didn't get busy until after three o'clock.

"Well, thanks for putting *that* idea in my head," Lana said after a beat. "Ugh." She looked around. "See anybody who could be a prisoner?"

"How would you know if they changed their clothes?" Annabelle asked.

"They would have that look," Lana replied. "You know the look I'm talking about."

When Annabelle didn't respond, Lana let loose an impatient gesture.

"You know the look," she insisted. "It's the gaze of a killer."

Hali wasn't thrilled at the notion of prisoners running all over St. Pete Beach and doing horrible things to survive, but she had to point out the flaw in Lana's logic. "Not all of them would be killers. I mean ... it's possible a few would be, but I think it's far more likely some were in there for drug charges, or theft. It wouldn't just be murder charges."

"I guess, but even one murderer is too many," Lana insisted.

Hali held out her hands. "Most of them were caught last night. My fear would be that the ones who escaped are the smart ones, and they won't be easy to capture going forward."

"Either they're the smart ones or they tripped over their

own dumb luck," Annabelle agreed. "It's hard to say. The ones who were graced by the dumb luck gods will be picked up first."

"The lead detective had breakfast with us this morning because he wanted to know what we saw," Hali volunteered. "He said they're announcing that any prisoner who turns herself in will not face additional charges for the escape."

"That's smart." Annabelle bobbed her head. "That should weed out a good three or four of them right there. Another two will be idiots who will get themselves caught right away. It's the last two or three who will be the issue."

"And I'm guessing those two or three will be the most dangerous inmates of all," Hali said.

"I think you're absolutely right," Annabelle agreed. "If they're smart, they're already out of this area. The ones still around will be caught relatively fast."

"You think the smart ones will flee?" Hali asked.

"Wouldn't you?"

Hali shrugged. "Actually, I would try to find a place to hole up. We're talking a place that has enough food to sustain me for a few days. Then I wouldn't leave that place. I would hunker down and keep hidden. I wouldn't emerge for at least a week."

"Because by then, everybody will assume that all the prisoners are out of this area," Annabelle surmised. "It's actually pretty smart."

"Andrew—he's the detective—said that they'll be staking out the known relatives and friends of the remaining prisoners," Hali explained. "I'm sure they'll catch one or two that way."

"The dumbest thing these guys can do is go home," Annabelle agreed. "When you're completely on your own, though, you don't have a lot of options. I can see a handful of them running to their mothers and being turned in. The parents aren't going to be idiots about it."

"Probably not." Hali leaned against the bar. Her mind was working overtime. "I can't imagine any of them coming down here because a prisoner is going to stick out like a sore thumb in this tourist crowd, but stranger things have happened."

"I'm surprised Gray isn't here to serve as your protector," Annabelle teased. "I thought for sure he would be camped out here for the entire week."

"He has some work stuff he has to tend to," Hali replied evasively. "I'm sure he's going to drop in again this afternoon. Right now, he's off with his brother."

"You almost seem relieved about that," Annabelle noted. "I hope there's no trouble in paradise."

"There's not," Hali replied. "We're good that way. I am happy he's off with his brother, though. Honestly, as much as I love spending time with him, he needs to get back into his regular routine. There is such a thing as too much quality time."

Annabelle's laugh was light. "So, basically he's doting a little too hard and you need room to breathe. That's what you're saying, isn't it?"

Hali hesitated, but not for long. "He can't give up his entire life for me. It's not healthy for him. We need balance. Both of us need it. For him, that includes time with his brother. For me, that includes running my bar."

"So, things are good?"

Before Hali could answer, Lana started in again.

"Fun fact," the effusive woman announced. "In Switzerland it's illegal to own one guinea pig. They're social animals, so if you try to adopt just one, it's considered animal abuse."

There was no hiding Hali's smile. "Things are good," she confirmed. "It feels like I'm slipping right back into my life."

"That's all that matters, right?" Annabelle prodded.

"I like having control," Hali confirmed. "It's all coming back to me now."

"Well, good for you."

"Thanks. I appreciate it."

6

SIX

The first tip on the list Harlan and Helene had bestowed upon Gray was a cabin near Madelaine Key. It was isolated, and Rusty and Gray parked a full mile away from their destination and hiked in. That allowed time for conversation.

"How is Hali?" Rusty asked. He recognized his brother had something heavy on his mind, but you couldn't come right out and ask Gray these things. You had to ease him into it. He was definitely the more intense Hunter brother.

"She's good." Gray's smile was soft. "She's so strong. She wants to be back to a hundred percent so badly."

"Was she ever at a hundred percent?"

"Before the accident. With me? Maybe not. She's always been perfect to me, though."

"Oh, so schmaltzy," Rusty teased. "You're just a big old bowl of marshmallow fluff for her, aren't you?"

"I'm going to ask her to marry me."

Rusty wasn't surprised. "Of course you are. When?"

"I don't know yet. I want to make a big deal out of it. I want her to be on solid footing with her hip. She was down a lot right before the surgery, and then immediately after. She's feeling better now. Even if her hip is never perfect again, she recognizes that she'll be better off now."

"That's good."

"It is."

"So, what has you so worked up?"

"You mean other than our mother trying to kill the woman I love?" Gray's tone was icy.

"I'm not going to make excuses for Mom," Rusty said. "There is no excuse for what she did. The thing is, she recognized she'd made a mistake, and she came forward. I don't want to say we should reward her for that—it's a strange word to throw around given what happened—but she did the right thing in the end."

"That wouldn't mean much if Hali had died."

"No, and I think she realizes that. She still ultimately did the right thing."

"You sound like Hali," Gray grumbled. "She wants me to forgive Mom."

"And you don't think you can?"

"Forgive her? I don't think that's in the cards. Can I move past it? I don't know. I can't even think on it much right now. There's other stuff going on."

"What other stuff?"

Gray told his brother about the prison break on the beach in halting terms. When he got to the part where the witch took him over, his stomach began to somersault. "I don't like the idea of knowing I could've hurt her," he said as he was finishing up. "I can't hurt her. She's my Hali."

Rusty had sympathy for his brother. The problem was, Gray was taking it to an extreme. That was Gray's way, though. "You didn't hurt her," he said in a gentle voice.

"I could have."

"Maybe, but Hali had things under control. She stopped you. She knows what she's doing and is strong. That's why you fell for her the way you did. Hali is just as strong as you."

"She wouldn't have killed me if she had to, though," Gray argued. "She would've sacrificed herself to protect me if it came to it."

"Do you want her to kill you?"

"No, but I want her to protect herself at all costs."

"Okay, but she loves you as much as you love her." Rusty used his most reasonable tone. "She's not going to sacrifice you to protect herself, just the same as you wouldn't sacrifice her to protect yourself."

"It's not the same."

"Why?" When Gray didn't immediately answer, a slow smile spread across Rusty's face. "It's because you have a penis, isn't it?"

Outrage clouded Gray's features. "Don't say it like that. I'm not sexist."

"You are a little. You can't expect Hali to do something that you wouldn't do yourself. That's the definition of sexism. You want to protect her because she's a woman. I mean ... it doesn't get more sexist than that."

Gray glared at him. "I am not sexist. I believe Hali can do anything I can do. In fact, I think Hali can do more than I can do. She's stronger than me."

"Okay." Rusty sounded utterly reasonable, which was why Gray knew that he was about to be annoyed. "Then why does Hali need to be protected more than you need to be protected?"

"Because I love her."

"And she loves you. Are you saying your love for her is greater than her love for you? Is it more important?"

"I…" Gray worked his jaw back and forth. "I'm done talking to you." He turned his back on his brother and kept trudging through the trees.

"Did I just win an argument?" Rusty excitedly scampered after his brother to catch up. "That has to be a first. I need a crown."

"Shut up," Gray barked.

"I definitely won." Rusty pumped his fist. "We should mark this day down in our calendars and celebrate it every year."

"I told you to shut up," Gray hissed. "You're bugging me."

"Oh, that just fuels me, and you know it," Rusty said. "I won today." His smile slipped when Gray pinned him with a death glare. "You have to let go of your guilt." He was serious now. "Hali did what she had to do. She protected you both. Don't treat her like an invalid. That will just turn her off over the long run."

"I'm not trying to treat her like an invalid," Gray countered. "I'm just trying to make sure that she's safe. I can't live without her. I know we haven't been together that long—"

"Long enough to know what you feel," Rusty countered. "You were a goner for her right from the start. That stuff just happens sometimes."

Gray sighed. "She's my life. I don't want her hurt. I would rather die than for something to happen to her."

"Well, that's great," Rusty said. "No, really and truly, I think it's great. You need to look at it from her point of view, though. She's not going to survive something bad happening to you. So, you guys are both going to need to learn about balance."

Gray didn't say anything. He registered the wisdom

associated with his brother's words, but he didn't want to admit it.

"I think Hali is having an easier time with that balance," Rusty said finally. "You've gotten used to doting on her over the past two weeks. As she gets stronger, you're going to have to pull back from that."

"I get it." Gray *did* get it. That didn't mean he had to like it. "I'm a sexist pig."

"It's more that you think your love is somehow greater than her love. It's not. I'm here to tell you that. You both love equally ... and it's humbling."

Gray's forehead creased. "Our love is humbling?"

"I never wanted to settle down and make a life with someone before I saw you and Hali together. Now I find myself wishing for what you have. It's definitely humbling."

"Aw, now I'm the one who needs a crown." Gray gave his brother a hearty shove. "Now, no more mush. Let's see if Russell is here."

"Do you think he is?" Rusty was all business now.

"I think it's unlikely," Gray replied. "We have to check, though. We'll know if he's been here. My guess is he isn't staying in one place. That's too dangerous. I bet he's jumping around."

"Right." Rusty nodded. "It makes the most sense. If he's already been here, maybe we can discern a pattern and get ahead of him eventually."

"I hope so. As long as Russell is still out there, he's a threat to us all."

"Yeah. We need to end that threat," Rusty agreed. "We can't move forward until we put the past behind us."

"Then let's see what we've got."

. . .

HALI HAD TO REST MORE OFTEN THAN SHE was comfortable with. She was feeling better, stronger, but too long standing made her hip ache like a rotten tooth. Thankfully, her workers weren't bringing it up. They seemed to realize she didn't want to acknowledge it.

Jesse was another story.

"Does it feel like your leg is going to come out of the socket?"

Hali glared at her brother. "Go bus some tables."

"It's hot out there," Jesse complained.

"Well, we are on the beach. And you're being paid. So, get out of my face."

Jesse made a grumbling noise as he headed out of the hut. "Thinks she can just sit there and boss me around," was the clearest thing Hali managed to make out.

"That's what happens when you're the boss," she called to his back.

Jesse being the typical little brother flipped her off without looking over his shoulder. Hali flipped him off right back, but he didn't see it. She muttered something about brothers being pains and then moved to the far window, the one closest to the building.

"What will it be?" she asked the woman on the stool. When she looked up, Hali almost came out of her skin because she recognized the woman. It was the witch from the previous evening. "What are you doing here?" she hissed.

Calmly, the witch glanced around. "You might want to lower your voice."

"And why would I want to do that?" Hali's annoyance was growing in leaps and bounds with each passing second.

"Because I don't believe—and I might be wrong here,

but I don't think I am—that you want to get into a magical free-for-all in front of your customers." The witch was positioned close to the fan, so the only person who could hear her was Hali.

Hali worked her jaw as she looked around the tiki bar. The regulars were sitting in the windows and chatting away with one another. There were tourists at the tables. Her brother was out complaining to anybody who would listen as he cleaned off other tables.

The witch was right. Hali couldn't risk a magical fight with so many innocents hanging around. On the other side of the bar, two local preppers she knew—both of whom liked to imbibe at all hours of the day—were lost in their own little world. If the witch were to put them under a spell as she had Gray, Hali knew things would take a terrible turn. Ed Craven and Benjamin Horton both took guns with them wherever they went.

"What will it be?" Hali gritted out.

"I'll take whatever that blue concoction is." The witch jerked her thumb toward Annabelle, who had a mermaid water daiquiri in front of her.

"Fine." Hali went about making it, although there was no finesse to what she was doing. She slammed the plastic cup down in front of the witch when she was finished. "That will be twelve bucks."

The witch smirked. "I think this one is on you." She sipped it and took on a far-off expression. "It's been two years since I've had anything this good."

"I'm pretty sure that's your fault," Hali replied. "You *are* the criminal."

"Except I'm not. I was falsely accused and convicted."

Hali had to hold back a harsh laugh. "Is that your story?"

"It is. My name is Angela Brennan. You can look me up."

Hali immediately reached for her phone.

"When I'm gone," Angela countered. "I don't have a lot of time. You can look me up after."

"After what?" Hali challenged.

"After I'm gone."

"Where are you going?" Hali did her best to appear breezy, but it wasn't easy. She was keyed up.

"You let me worry about that." Angela's smile was smug. "I'm not saying I don't trust you ... but I don't trust you."

"You shouldn't trust me," Hali readily agreed. "If I didn't have customers here right now, you would already be down and out."

"So sure of yourself."

"I am."

"I guess you have the pedigree to back it up." Angela took another sip of her drink. "I did some research on you after our ... *unfortunate incident* ... last night."

"Is that what you're calling it?" Hali was haughty. "An unfortunate incident? You tried to make my boyfriend kill me."

"Not kill you. I just wanted you out of the way. You were working too fast. I wasn't expecting a witch to be on the beach. I was the one who directed everybody down there because I thought it was my best bet of escape. I had no idea we would be up against you."

"Am I supposed to feel flattered about that?" Hali glared. "For the record, I don't."

"I don't expect you to feel flattered," Angela replied. "In your shoes, I would be just as angry. I had to do what I had to do, though."

"You mean take over my boyfriend and rape his mind."

"That's an interesting word choice." Angela didn't deny it. "I knew you were powerful. I was just trying to distract you. I needed to get away."

"And now what?" Hali challenged. "What's the plan now? What are you going to do?"

"I'm going to convince you to clear my name."

Whatever she was expecting, that wasn't it. Hali's mouth fell open, and she burst out laughing. Several sets of eyes flicked to her from around the bar—it was rare for her to laugh like that—but she smiled and shrugged before turning back to Angela. "I have no interest in clearing your name."

"The big witch on the beach, the one who is called a do-gooder by all the paranormals, doesn't want to right a wrong?" Angela challenged. "That doesn't seem accurate."

Hali narrowed her eyes. "Maybe I don't believe you were wrongly convicted."

"You don't even know anything about me." Angela was calm, but she was also hyper-vigilant. She followed every shadow with her eyes, and Hali recognized she was ready to bolt should the need arise. "I've been locked away for two years, and for something I didn't do. You're going to help me prove I was wrongly convicted."

Hali had no idea what to make of the situation. "And why would I want to do that?"

"Because you can't stand an injustice. You're the big hero of the beach. It wasn't hard to figure out who you were last night. Once I had access to the internet, all I had to do was type in 'St. Pete Beach witch' and you were right there. You're a regular topic in all the chat rooms."

Hali had questions about that. Now didn't seem like the time to ask them, though. "If you say so. I'm not helping you, though."

"And why not? Are you suggesting, just because I was in prison, that I don't deserve the same level of help you would offer others?"

"You took over my boyfriend and tried to make him hurt me. Do you have any idea how haunted he is by that?"

"He shouldn't even remember it."

"That doesn't matter. He knows because I told him. He's very upset."

"Well, he didn't hurt you. You hurt him." Angela was matter of fact. "That should count for something."

"I didn't want to hurt him." Hali's temper flared again. "I'm not helping you."

"Yes, you are." Angela didn't back down. "You're going to do exactly what I want you to do."

"No."

"You'll do it, or I'll come back and take over your boyfriend again. This time, I'll make it so you have to kill him if you want to save yourself."

Hali's heart thudded hard. She didn't like what the witch was saying. Even more, she didn't like the serious look on the woman's face. She could tell the witch meant business. "If you go near Gray, I'll kill you." She meant every word of it.

"Except I can attack from afar and you won't even see me coming," Angela replied. "You *are* going to help me."

Frustration reared up and grabbed Hali by the heart. "Or what?"

"I just told you what will happen if you don't. Pretend you have a say in the matter. Pretend you want to help me."

"Yeah, that's not really how I operate," Hali countered. "I don't like it when people back me into corners."

"Welcome to the club." Angela took another sip of her

cocktail. "My life hasn't turned out how I thought it would. I've been wrongly accused. You are going to help me prove it. In exchange, I promise to leave your boyfriend alone. If I need a big, strong shifter to protect myself, I won't go after him."

There was nothing about that statement Hali liked. "Or how about you don't go after anyone. It's not fair to use mind magic on the unwilling."

"We both know I can't make that promise," Angela replied evenly. "It's simply impossible. If I get backed into a corner, then I'll use whatever magic is necessary to get myself out. It is what it is."

Hali narrowed her eyes. "Where would I even start if I wanted to clear you?"

"Well, according to the stories I read last night, you're pretty good at doing the police's job for them. You've solved quite a few mysteries, right here on the beach. All I'm asking is that you do the same for me."

"But—"

"No." Angela shook her head to cut off Hali. "You're doing it." She drained the rest of her drink and stood. "If you don't, I'll come back and I'll make you wish you had. If your boyfriend doesn't want to be used, then you're going to have to make sure it doesn't happen. You're the one in control here."

Hali glanced around again. It was obvious Angela was leaving. There was nothing she could do to stop it either. If she called attention to Angela, the others would try to help. They could end up hurt—or worse—in the process. On top of that, Hali couldn't use her magic in front of this particular audience. She wasn't exactly on the down low when it came to her powers. Normal humans weren't privy to what she could do, though.

"And how do I get in touch with you when I've managed to prove your innocence?" she asked finally.

"Don't worry about that," Angela replied. "I'll be in touch with you." She turned to leave and then stopped herself. "Don't do anything stupid, Hali Waverly. I get that you're powerful. I'm powerful too. Unlike you, though, I have nothing to lose. Love is a weakness."

Hali glared at her. "If you believe that, then you've never truly been in love."

"You don't know anything about me. You should do a bit of research. Something tells me you're smart enough to figure things out. When you do, I'll know. Then I'll be in touch again."

"Wait." Hali was desperate as she tried to stop her. "You can't just drop this on me and go."

A small smile played at the corners of Angela's mouth. "I can do whatever I want. You're the one who doesn't have choices." She turned and offered up a haphazard wave over her shoulder. "I'll be seeing you soon."

Hali glowered at her retreating back. Just what was she supposed to do here?

7
SEVEN

Hali was at a loss. She knew she had to report seeing Angela—there were cameras everywhere on the Paradise Lodge grounds—but she didn't know what the smartest move was. Ultimately, she called Andrew because she trusted him more than she trusted anyone else on the police force.

Andrew didn't look happy to be summoned out to the Paradise Lodge grounds yet again when he arrived. One look at Hali had him switching up his attitude.

"Are you okay?" He sat on the same stool Angela had vacated. "What happened?"

Hali filled a cup with iced tea with no prodding and slid it to him. She filled him in on her conversation with Angela in halting terms, and when she was finished, she was still spitting mad. "So, that's where we're at."

"Have you looked up Angela Brennan?"

"I tried googling her, but that name is fairly common."

"Right." Andrew pulled out his phone. "Angela Brennan is on the list of prisoners who are still out there," he said after a few seconds. "It looks like she was convicted of killing a man in her apartment building."

Hali's forehead creased. "Just some random guy?"

"Um ... hold on. I'm trying to pull up the specifics." Andrew's forehead was creased in concentration. "It looks like he was an ex-boyfriend, or at least that's what they argued in court. His name was Seth Rochester. He had a very long rap sheet that includes armed robbery, domestic violence, and even charges of stalking...although he was never convicted of that."

"I once read it's virtually impossible to bring stalking charges against people," Hali volunteered. "Even celebrities have a hard time."

"They do have a hard time," Andrew confirmed. "I'm of the mind that stalking laws should be enhanced—it's a terrible crime that can wear on someone mentally, almost like being gaslit in public over and over again—but I don't have a say in the matter."

"So, what was Seth's relationship with Angela?" Hali was determined to understand the nuance of what she was dealing with before making a decision either way on what she was going to do.

"They lived in the same building." Andrew kept reading. "Neighbors said they were romantically involved, but also had a business arrangement."

"What sort of business?"

"Drugs."

Hali's stomach clenched. "What sort of drugs?"

"Meth it looks like. Pot. Um ... there's mention of heroin but that wasn't found in Seth's apartment."

"And what happened to Seth?" Hali found she didn't want to know the details but had no choice. If she was going to help Angela—and that wasn't something she wanted to do—she was going to have to know everything about the woman there was to know.

"He was stabbed."

Hali waited. She knew there was more to the story.

"Six times," Andrew added. "In the back."

Hali scowled. "Lovely. And why did they assume it was Angela? Obviously, Seth was the sort of guy who had more than one cohort."

"Cohort." Andrew chuckled. "That's a good word. You're right, though. Seth was known to have multiple associates. None of them were good. Angela apparently moved out of her apartment the day after he was killed—but a full day before he was discovered—and that was deemed suspicious."

"It could be that she just knew he'd been killed," Hali argued. "That doesn't necessarily mean she did the deed. They must have had evidence."

"Um ... her fingerprints were found in the apartment."

"If they were dating, wouldn't that be normal?"

Andrew shrugged. "Yes. Everything I see in this file is circumstantial."

"And how long was she sentenced to?"

"Fifteen years."

"That doesn't seem like much for killing somebody."

"It really doesn't," he agreed. "She went down for second-degree, not first-degree. Apparently, the prosecutors didn't think they had enough evidence for first-degree charges."

Hali pressed her lips together. "Angela said she wouldn't leave Gray alone unless I proved her innocence."

"Okay, but that doesn't actually mean she's innocent, Hali. She could be after you to manufacture evidence or something. I mean … what does she expect you to do? You're not a cop."

"She said I'm a celebrity in local paranormal chat groups."

"I can see that."

"She said that I helped others, so I had to help her."

"And what do you want to do?"

Hali was thrown by the question. "I can't let anything happen to Gray."

Andrew rolled his eyes. "You two are going to get yourselves in trouble if you're not careful. You're both far too willing to fall on swords—imaginary and real—to protect one another. You need to stop that."

"I'll do whatever is necessary to protect Gray." Hali was adamant. "I'll die before I let anything happen to him."

"See, that right there is what I'm talking about." Andrew jabbed a finger at her. "Nobody is dying."

"Then what do we do?"

Andrew took advantage of the iced tea as a distraction and sipped as he thought about it. "We could talk to Angela's cellmate. I just checked, and she was one of the ones who was captured. It was already on my list to talk to the cellmates of those who managed to escape. If we dangle a carrot, she might just jump on it."

Hali didn't have to consider it long. "You drive."

He smirked. "Don't you want to call Gray and tell him what you're doing?"

Hali was appalled and offended by the suggestion. "He's not my boss."

Andrew glanced around. "Where is he? I would've thought, since it's your first day back, that he would be here, glued to your side."

"He had things to do." Hali averted her gaze.

Andrew wasn't an idiot. He'd been friends with Gray since they were kids. "Hali."

"Fine." Her eyes flashed with annoyance. "He's with Rusty. Harlan and Helene showed up after breakfast trying to make amends. They had a list of possible locations where Russell might be found."

"And what do they plan on doing if they find him?"

"I don't think they plan on killing him, if that's what you're worried about," Hali assured him. "It's far more likely they'll drag him in front of the pack and let them decide how to deal with him."

"That doesn't make me feel any better. I still think you should call Gray."

"Well, I'm not." Hali vehemently shook her head. "It's not as if I'm not going to tell him. I don't want him getting worked up right now, though. This is the first time he's left me in weeks. He needs the time out with his brother."

"And you need the time to figure things out before you break the bad news to him," Andrew surmised. "I get it."

"He's not going to take it well." Hali gripped her hands together in front of her. "He's going to be upset."

"Do you blame him?"

"No. It's not his fault, though."

"It's not yours either."

"I didn't say it was my fault. It's my responsibility now, though." She took a steadying breath. "One way or another."

Andrew stared at her for several seconds, then nodded. "We'll head out to the prison. We'll talk to the cellmate. That's all I can commit to at this point."

"That's enough for me. I just need an idea of what I'm dealing with here. All we know so far is that Angela might or might not have killed a drug dealer."

"Her choice of victim doesn't make her a good person."

"Oh, I'm under no illusion that she's a good person." Hali was grim. "She's a survivor—that's obvious—but even if she were framed, she's not a good person."

"Okay." Andrew drained the rest of his iced tea and stood. "Let's get this over with. If Gray is mad, though, I'm totally blaming it all on you."

"I can live with that."

"You say that now. You might not feel the same way in three hours."

"One step at a time."

"Then let's go. I'll drive. You're going to need your identification. I plan to introduce you as a consultant, but you still need to prove your identity."

Hali nodded. "No problem." She grabbed her purse. "Let me just tell Jesse he's in charge again—something that will make him extremely happy—and then we're out of here."

"That sounds like a plan to me."

ZEPHYRHILLS CORRECTIONAL WAS A FORMER MALE-ONLY prison that now had a women's wing. Hali had never much thought about the institution, even though it was only forty-five minutes away from St. Pete Beach.

During the ride with Andrew, they talked about what it was like growing up with Gray as a friend. Andrew had funny stories—and Hali wanted to hear all of them—but the closer they got to the prison, the more anxious she got.

"Nobody is going to try to shiv me, right?" she asked.

Andrew let loose a low chuckle. "No. You're not going to be anywhere near the cells. I'm having the cellmate—one Penelope Richards—brought to an interrogation room. It will be fine. She'll be cuffed."

"And what did Penelope Richards do?" Hali asked.

"She caught her husband cheating with her mother and killed him."

Hali's eyebrows hiked up her forehead. "Her husband cheated with her mother? That's gross." She tried to picture Gray with her mother and came up with a horrifying scenario. "So very gross."

Andrew chuckled. "According to Penelope, she was going to kill her mother too, but she managed to climb out a window. She shot the husband and tried to chase her mother around the neighborhood, but the cops caught her before she could do any damage."

"That's just a terrible thing to happen."

"You're so pretty." Andrew grinned at her as he pulled up to the guard shack. "You can't see ugliness in the world. It ruins your whole day."

"I've seen ugliness."

"You have, but you live and work on a beach. Your life is just brighter and shinier by design."

Hali didn't know what to make of that, so she just nodded. "I guess."

Andrew showed his identification to the man in the guard tower and waited for confirmation to head inside. Once they entered the building, Hali had to hand over her identification, just as Andrew had warned. The process to check in took a full thirty minutes, and when they were finished, she was frazzled.

"That's a lot of hoops to jump through," she complained. "Shouldn't you be able to just flash your badge and be done?"

"Yeah, cops have gone bad in the past and developed romantic relationships with prisoners," he explained. "We have as many safeguards in place to protect from that as possible."

"And yet that one female guard managed to escape with a male prisoner a few years ago."

"They were caught, though."

"I guess."

Hali and Andrew were situated in the conference room first. Two guards brought Penelope Richards in five minutes later. She was in the same orange jumpsuit Hali recognized from the night before, and her hands and ankles were shackled. She had to shuffle inside the room.

"Sit," one of the guards ordered.

Penelope did as she was told. Her hair was wild and dark, as if it hadn't been brushed in days. She had on heavy makeup, which Hali didn't understand. The last thing she would care about if in prison was perfect eyeliner and mascara. Also ... was makeup even allowed in prison? The woman's eyes sparkled as she glanced between Hali and Andrew. She looked excited about what was to come.

"Are you here to offer me a deal?" she asked once the guards had vacated the space.

"That depends," Andrew replied. "What are you going to give me in return?"

"What do you want?" Penelope seemed ready to wheel and deal. "I don't do hand jobs no more because I've been screwed on that front too many times. Once the hand job is over with, I never seem to get my promised reward."

Andrew made a face. "Nobody is here for a hand job."

Penelope's eyes moved to Hali. "You have that covered for him?"

"Um ... no." Hali owned a bar. She was used to crude conversation, especially as the day wore on. She felt out of her element here. "I let Andrew handle that for himself."

"I'm not here for sexual favors," Andrew replied. "I'm here because I want to know about your cellmate."

Penelope was a calculating individual. She straightened at the news, cocked her head, and glanced between them. "I understand why you're here," she said to Andrew. "You're trying to find Angela. When I heard she was still on the loose, I figured I would be getting a visit. What I don't get is why you're here." Her eyes landed on Hali. "What do you have to do with Angela?"

"I met her last night," Hali replied. She was careful when choosing her words. "I was on the beach when you guys made it down there ... although I don't remember seeing you."

"Yeah, I didn't make it to the beach," Penelope said. "They got me on the street. I thought it would be smarter to go in the opposite direction as everybody else. Turns out that was the wrong decision to make."

"Sounds like it." Hali shot her a rueful smile. "I'm sorry you got caught so soon."

Penelope let loose a harsh laugh. "Them's the breaks. You can't miss what you didn't even know you had. I didn't even get a chance to dream about freedom before it was over. Besides, the only thing I want to do is finish what I started, and I don't even know where my mother is right now. I was never going to make it to her."

Hali didn't have any idea how to respond to that, so she remained quiet.

"We want specifics on Angela," Andrew prodded. "In exchange, I'll tell the prosecutor you were helpful and ask that you not face additional charges for the jailbreak."

"They're not going to charge me for the jailbreak anyway," Penelope countered. "I was just wandering around and got lost. I wasn't that far from the bus. They won't charge me because it won't be worth their time."

"Then what do you want?" Andrew challenged.

"I'm guessing you can't get time off my initial sentence."

"No, I cannot. I wouldn't offer that anyway. You're obviously still a danger."

Rather than take offense at the statement, Penelope grinned. "I'm totally a danger. Drop fifty in my commissary and I'll tell you whatever you want."

"Fifty bucks?" Andrew looked torn.

"I'll cover it," Hali offered out of the blue. "You're helping me. I don't expect you to pay it."

"We're helping each other," Andrew said. "We can handle the commissary, though," he promised Penelope. "I'll see to it before I leave."

"Then I'm your girl." Penelope's smile was so wide it stretched across her entire face. "Tell me what you want to know."

"Well, for starters, do you have any idea where Angela would go?" Andrew had produced a small notebook from his suit pocket and was poised to start writing.

"Angela didn't have anybody to go to on the outside," Penelope replied. "She hadn't heard from her mother in ages. We're talking since before she went to prison. She said her mother was a druggie whore and they had nothing to do with one another."

"What about her father?" Hali asked.

"Her pops took off when she was five or something. She said he contacted her when he went to prison. She was a teenager at the time. He wanted money. She didn't give him any—for obvious reasons... I mean, you don't help a deadbeat who is very clearly using you—and he was mad. That was the last time they spoke."

"What about a boyfriend?" Andrew asked. "I know she was convicted of killing her boyfriend, but sometimes you find new ones, even if you're behind bars."

"Angela had a few boyfriends," Penelope confirmed. "They all put money in her commissary. I don't have names, though. She came up with nicknames, though. Like Two-Stroke. When they had phone sex, he lasted two strokes. There was Pinprick too. I think we all know where that name came from."

"So, if I check her commissary account, I might come up with a few names," Andrew guessed.

Penelope nodded. "Yeah. They all sounded like dregs to me. They just wanted the phone sex and to be able to say they had a girlfriend. I'm not sure any of them would've helped her, and I'm even less certain that they would be gutsy enough to put her up if she showed up on their doorsteps."

Andrew nodded. "You must have some idea where she would go. You guys were cellmates for two years. You must've talked."

"We did and we didn't," Penelope replied. "I wouldn't say we were friends, but when you're stuck in close quarters with someone for such a long time, there's no choice but to become friendly. She didn't confide in me. She did rant, though."

Andrew cocked an eyebrow. "And what did she rant about?"

"She kept saying over and over again that she was innocent, and she was being framed. That was her mantra for a long time. Everybody says that, though, so nobody thinks much of it. One day I asked, even though I didn't care. I wanted to know who set her up.

"Like me, for example, I don't bother with the 'they set me up' storyline because I can't sell that," she continued. "I still had the gun in my hand when they caught me ... and I'm not sorry I put that piece of crap down. I only wish I'd caught my mother before the cops got there. That's another rant, though.

"As for Angela, she claimed she didn't do it and she was set up by someone specific," Penelope explained. "She never dropped the facade even once, so I kind of believe her."

"Well, don't leave us hanging," Andrew said. "Who did she say set her up?"

"Her twin sister. I think her name is Camila or something. She goes by Cammie, though."

Andrew shot a quick look toward Hali. "I didn't realize she had a twin sister. I don't remember reading that in her file."

"I think they were separated into different foster homes a lot when they were growing up," Penelope replied. "Their mom was even worse than my mom."

"What can you tell us about Cammie?" Andrew asked.

"Apparently, she was a skank, and Angela hated her. They were in competition for the dead guy or something. At least that's what Angela said. Supposedly, Cammie killed that dealer knowing that Angela would get blamed for it. If I were looking for Angela, I would start with Cammie. She's going to find her one way or another."

Andrew leaned back in his chair, taking it all in. "Can you think of anything else?" he asked finally.

Penelope shook her head. "No. Do I get my commissary?"

Hali nodded before Andrew could respond. "You do," she said. "You earned it. Thank you."

"No problem." Penelope remained seated as Hali and Andrew stood. "When you catch Angela, don't tell her I told on her. She won't be happy."

"We'll keep it to ourselves," Andrew promised. "Thank you for your time."

"No, thank you. I'm going to buy some candy bars just as soon as my money comes through. That will be the highlight of my week."

Hali tried not to dwell on how sad that made her. "I'll put the money in right now. Thank you so much."

"You're not so bad," Penelope said. "You're out of your element, but you're not so bad."

"Thanks. I think." Hali flashed a hesitant smile. "You're not so bad either."

"Tell my mother that."

"Yes, well, I think I'll stay out of that one."

Penelope chuckled. "That's the smartest thing you could do. Trust me."

8
EIGHT

Because they were already passing through Tampa on their way back to St. Pete Beach, Hali and Andrew stopped at the Brennan residence on their way home. Andrew warned Hali not to say anything—*I'm not Gray, and you're not my official sidekick*—and she tried not to be offended. Andrew could tell her nose was out of joint, though.

"I'm sorry," he said in a low voice as they stood at the front door. "I could get in trouble for having you with me."

Hali tried not to be bothered by his words, but she was. "I'm not Gray's sidekick. He's mine."

Andrew blinked several times. "That's what you're upset about?" he asked dumbly.

"I don't want to be the sidekick."

Andrew was caught between amusement and disbelief. "Well, I'm sorry I made you the sidekick." Really, what else was he supposed to say? "It won't happen again."

"Thank you." Hali plastered a pretty smile on her face when the door opened to reveal a raggedy couple in their late forties.

The woman wasn't wearing pants, just a long T-shirt that barely covered her rear end. As for the man, he was shirtless and had doughnut crumbs all over his chest. He also appeared to be wearing pink vented shorts that were clearly two sizes too small, something she recognized because she was almost positive she received two glimpses of things she didn't want to see hanging out from beneath the shorts. That had her pinning her gaze on the ceiling above the door, which also turned out to be a mistake because there was a wasp nest up there.

"What do you want?" the woman asked. She didn't look happy about being interrupted.

"Are you Laura Brennan?" Andrew asked. He kept his face neutral.

"So what if I am? Who are you?"

"He's a cop," the man said in a low voice. "He's got cop written all over him. So does the woman."

Hali frowned. "I'm not a cop."

"But you're right about me being a police officer." Andrew flashed his badge because it was procedure. He could tell right away that these people didn't care about procedure, though. They just wanted him gone. He decided to use that to his advantage. "I don't want to take up much of your time, but I'm sure you're aware that Angela escaped last night."

"We heard." Laura scratched her cheek. "She's not here."

"Do you mind if we look around?" Andrew asked.

Laura opened her mouth, then shut it. "Do you have a warrant?"

"I do not."

"Well, I think you need a warrant." She darted a worried look toward the man, who Hali was still eyeing with a great deal of trepidation. "Right, Rick? He needs a warrant."

Rick fervently nodded. "Don't let him in, Laura," he hissed. "They'll frame us and blame us for whatever Angela has done."

Andrew held up his hands in supplication. "Nobody has any intention of framing or blaming you," he assured them. "In fact, if there's any contraband in the house, I'm willing to overlook it if you let me search for Angela."

Laura's interest was clearly piqued. "What sort of contraband are you talking about?"

"Drugs," Andrew replied without hesitation. "I'm not here about any drugs. I don't care about the drugs at present. I'm just trying to find Angela."

Laura's tongue took a slow walk around her lips as she debated. "Do you promise?" she asked finally.

"I'm not vice," Andrew assured her. "I'm just looking for the missing prisoners."

"Fine." Laura held open the door. "If you screw me, I'm going to be mad though."

"That seems more than fair." Andrew ushered Hali in front of him. He didn't touch her lower back as Gray might under similar circumstances, but he did remain protectively close.

The house was a nondescript ranch that had seen better days. There were burn holes in the carpet. To Hali, it looked as if someone had punched a fist through the drywall at some point and then hadn't bothered to fix it. Andrew pointed toward the hallway, and Hali stood there while he checked the two bedrooms down the hallway. He was shaking his head when he returned to Hali.

"She's not here."

"No, she's not," Hali agreed. If Angela were here, Hali

would've been able to sense her magic. The other witch had taken her by surprise at the tiki bar earlier, but Hali hadn't been actively searching for potential enemies at the time. Now she was, and there was no sign of Angela. There was, however, a big pile of pot on the living room table.

"You can't touch us," Rick reminded Andrew as they sat on the couch and chairs.

"I don't have interest in your pot," Andrew assured him. "Although, seriously, just put it in a drawer or something." He looked pained. "I might not be the only police officer stopping by. At some point the U.S Marshalls are going to get involved, and they'll be here. Other local or state officials might stop by. You guys should be prepared."

"Good tip." Laura beamed at him. "I like you."

"Hey!" Rick was clearly offended. "I'm right here."

Andrew held up his hand to stop the potential argument. "Rick—that's what she called you, right?—what's your last name?"

"I don't have one," Rick lied. The way he darted his eyes to the left told Hali he was lying. Of course, she didn't need to see the tell to recognize that.

"Rick, just tell me," Andrew argued. "I need to know."

"Rick Simmons," Laura replied.

"Laura!" Rick's eyes looked as if they were going to bug out of his head. "You don't tell 'the Man' nothing. What did I tell you when we first hooked up?"

Andrew exchanged an amused look with Hali. While Rick and Laura clearly had issues, they also didn't appear to be a threat.

"None of this is my fault," Laura complained. "I'm just trying to help. I mean ... he's the police, and he seems like one of the few good ones."

"When was the last time you saw Angela?" Andrew asked. He was desperate to keep the conversation on track.

"Oh, well ... it's been a long time." Laura's forehead creased in concentration. "I lost custody of her a few times when she was a teenager. I tried to make amends, but Angela didn't want anything to do with me.

"That's no skin off my nose," she continued. "I don't need to waste time on anybody who doesn't love me. It's not my fault I was chased by the demon of alcohol for so long. I've finally kicked that habit, but Angela doesn't care."

Hali's eyes immediately went to the beer cans that were strewn around the room.

"That's just beer," Laura explained. "I kicked liquor, not beer."

Hali had questions—oh, so many questions—but she wisely kept them to herself.

"What do you know about Angela's conviction?" Andrew asked.

"Which one?"

"The one where she was convicted of killing her boyfriend," Andrew replied. "I know she got picked up a few times as a teenager for solicitation and some misdemeanor drug charges, but I'm more interested in the big crime."

"I didn't know that guy," Laura replied. "I think I saw him maybe twice. Both times I stopped by to try to talk to Angela—I thought she could loan me a few bills—but she always refused. She had a bug up her butt about her childhood."

"Meaning what?" Andrew prodded.

"Meaning that she was convinced that I was a bad mother. As if. Most mothers wouldn't have even kept her. I told her I could've aborted her. I thought about it. She's lucky I didn't. It would've been easier for me."

Hali had to hold back a wince. The last thing she wanted was to feel sorry for Angela—the woman was actively threatening Gray after all—but seeing what the witch had likely grown up with, she couldn't help herself. Laura was a mess.

"Are you Angela's father?" Andrew asked Rick.

"Me?" Rick looked horrified at the thought. "No way."

"That was Henry Johnson," Laura volunteered. "He took off when they were toddlers. He was the reason I had them in the first place—he said it was a sin to get rid of them—but did he hang around and help?"

"I'm guessing not," Hali said blandly.

"Definitely not," Laura agreed. "He wasn't there. Only I was there. Those girls should've understood I was doing the best I could."

She'd given them the opening, so Andrew walked through it. "What can you tell me about Angela's relationship with Cammie?" he asked.

"They were sisters," Laura replied. "Twins."

"I know that part." Andrew had to tug on his limited patience to keep from exploding. "Were they close?"

Hali had another question. "Were they identical?"

"Oh, they were little clones." Laura bobbed her head. "It was freaky. I left their hospital bracelets identifying them on for a month when I brought them home because I was afraid of mixing them up. Finally, I had no choice but to cut them off because they were cutting off circulation, and I didn't want their little hands to fall off. After that, I tried to remember to draw on them with marker, but that didn't always work. It's possible they're not going by the right names even now."

Hali cocked her head. "I see." She glanced at Andrew, who looked as baffled as she felt.

"I've gone through Angela's files," Andrew said, drawing Laura's attention back to him. "It says here that the girls were removed from your care six times over the course of their lives. The first time was when they were three. They were taken in by a nice family right here in Tampa. The family wanted to adopt them, but you managed to get them back before that could happen."

"That's right." Laura looked proud of herself. "You don't just abandon your kids."

Hali couldn't help wondering how much better things might've been for Cammie and Angela if they'd been adopted by a good family. Laura might not have been the worst person in the world, but she wasn't a good parent either. Maybe things would've been different for the twins if Laura had done the selfless thing and given them up. Money didn't buy happiness but love and stability did.

"They were removed from your home again when they were five—"

"I was framed for that robbery," Laura insisted.

"And eight," Andrew added. "And twelve. Then the final time they were removed from your home was when they were sixteen."

"As you can tell, those social workers just wanted to harass me," Laura complained.

"Yes, it was obviously all somebody else's fault," Andrew agreed darkly.

Laura shot him a dirty look. "I was a good mother."

Andrew didn't respond to the charge. "The final time the girls were put into foster care, Cammie went to a woman in St. Pete and Angela went to a group home. Do you know why that is?"

"Is it important?" Laura asked.

"It could be." Andrew kept his face neutral, but it took effort.

"Well, the social worker asked me what I thought for their placement," Laura explained. "It's always hard to place older kids. I was annoyed at the time because Angela had gotten into my stash and sold it to her teacher for a passing grade, so I thought a little payback was in order."

Hali felt sick to her stomach but didn't react. The effort it took to keep her face placid was off the charts, though.

"I told the social worker that Cammie was a dream, and that Angela was troubled," Laura continued. She either didn't see how bad she was coming off or didn't care. Hali had no idea which. "That's one of those words social workers like to use. *Troubled.* Basically, I made it so Cammie got a good placement and Angela got a bad one."

"Are you proud of that?" Hali asked without thinking. She ignored the warning look Andrew shot her.

"Why shouldn't I be?" Laura challenged. "Angela needed to learn boundaries. The girl never did. She was always a handful. Cammie was the good one. She deserved the reward for being the good one."

Hali had a feeling that Cammie was considered the good one because she always kowtowed to Laura's wishes. Angela was stronger, and likely stood up for herself more, and Laura didn't like that.

"Do you believe Angela killed the man she's accused of killing?" Andrew asked.

"Sure." Laura didn't look bothered by the question. "She's a survivor. She would kill if she had to. That's who she is."

"But do you think she killed this particular man?" Andrew pressed.

"I don't know. You guys seem to think so. That's good enough for me."

"What about Cammie?" Andrew pressed. "Are she and Angela still close?"

"I don't think so." Laura shook her head. "Things have never been the same since that last time they were taken. Cammie was with those people for two years. They helped her focus on her schoolwork. She actually got decent grades there at the end and managed to go to community college." Laura looked legitimately impressed. "I heard she works at a bank now or something, although I guess I haven't seen her in five years or so. Not just as a teller. She does mortgages and makes good money."

"But you don't see her?" Andrew asked.

Laura shook her head. "She thinks she's better than me now. Last time I ran into her, she acted embarrassed."

"Were you wearing pants?" Hali asked before she could stop herself.

Andrew shot her a quelling look, but his lips quirked, telling Hali he was fighting the urge to laugh.

"Cammie ended up fine," Laura replied. "She should be thanking me. Angela turned out to be a deadbeat. Nobody is surprised. She inherited that from her daddy."

"Yes, obviously none of it came from you," Hali muttered.

Andrew lightly patted Hali's forearm to get her to shut up. "What about Cammie and Angela, though? Are you telling me they completely severed ties?"

Laura held her hands palms out. "As far as I know, they don't talk any longer. Angela was jealous that Cammie had a good final family—Cammie is still in touch with them, or was last I knew—and she tried to drag Cammie into trouble. Cammie refused. Angela got her nose out of joint."

Laura leaned forward, as if imparting a great secret on them. "Cammie didn't even show up when Angela was on trial. I did, though. I was there for my girl ... not that she thanked me or anything. A few of the local television stations tossed me a few bucks for interviews, though, so it was all worth it."

"It sounds as if it was all worth it," Andrew said dryly. "Can you think of any reason Angela would want to go after Cammie?"

"She's been jealous of her for years at this point," Laura replied. "It's hard to tell what she'll do. I'm sure prison didn't help matters."

"To your knowledge, did Cammie visit Angela in prison?"

"No." Laura shook her head. "Why would she? Angela made her own mistakes. It wasn't Cammie's job to fix them. You can't reason with Angela. She's crazy. She doesn't care who she hurts as long as she's okay."

"I wonder where she got that from," Hali muttered under her breath.

"Her father," Laura answered without hesitation. "He was a terrible parent."

Andrew worked his jaw before glancing at Hali. There was really nothing else to do here. "Thank you for your time," he said as he stood. "Clean up the drugs. I'm betting you'll get another visitor, especially if Angela isn't captured today. Try to do yourself a favor and not get in trouble, huh?"

"Thanks for the tip, man." Rick mock saluted him.

"Yes, well, I aim to please." Andrew was quiet until they were back in his vehicle. "What do you think?" he asked Hali.

"I think Angela never had a shot thanks to her parents." She was morose.

"Do you think she's innocent, though?"

That question was harder for Hali to answer. "I have no idea. We need to find the sister."

"Yeah. I've started a search. There's nothing active on her Social Security number for years, so that bank job is no more. Hopefully, we'll find her sooner rather than later. If I were her, though, I would've changed my name and moved out of the area."

"Do you think she did that?"

"I have no idea."

GRAY WAS FRUSTRATED AFTER A FRUITLESS day of searching for Russell—they'd checked five locations and come up empty five times—so he was in a poor mood when he showed up at Hali's tiki bar. That mood only darkened further when he realized she was nowhere to be found.

"Where is Hali?" Gray demanded as he rested his elbows on the bar and leaned in to catch Jesse's gaze.

"What?" Jesse looked frazzled. He didn't work well under pressure.

"Did she need a nap?" Gray asked. His stomach lurched at the prospect. "She didn't have to go back to the doctor, did she?" He was going to be mad at himself if Hali needed medical care and he wasn't around to help.

"Oh, she's fine." Jesse waved his hand. "At least she was when she left with your detective friend this afternoon."

It was not the response Gray was anticipating. "What now?" he demanded.

"That friend of yours. The cop."

"Andrew Copeland," Gray confirmed.

"Yeah. She called him, and he was out here fast. They talked in low voices for a bit and then took off together." Something occurred to Jesse. "It didn't look romantic or anything."

Gray made a face. He wasn't worried in the least about Hali cheating. She just didn't have it in her. She was capable of throwing herself headlong into danger if the mood struck, however.

"Why did she call Andrew?" Gray asked. He was trying to work it all out in his head.

"I'm not sure." Jesse's shoulders hopped. "Some woman sat over there." He pointed toward the last stool on the left side of the bar. "She and Hali talked for several minutes. Hali seemed upset. Then the woman left, and Hali called the cop."

"And you didn't think to go and check why your sister was upset?" Gray demanded.

"No way. She's been cranky ever since her surgery. I don't need her negativity."

Gray threw his hands up in the air. "You're unbelievable."

"Thank you," Jesse said. "Does this mean you're going to take over so I can have a break?"

"No," Gray replied. "It means you're going to work the final hour of your shift—you didn't even work eight hours today, Jesse, for crying out loud—and then you're going to take off and do what you want. That's what normal people do when it comes to having a job."

"I don't think I like being a normal person," Jesse complained.

"Join the club, kid. Being an adult is hard. You've barely gotten into it. I have bad news. It's going to get worse."

Jesse looked horrified. "It can't possibly get worse."

"Buckle up, Buttercup. You've had it easy until now. You're facing a hard adjustment, and I can't wait to see you take it on."

"But ... this bites," Jesse complained. "I want to go back to my old life."

"Tough." Gray pushed himself away from the tiki bar. "I'm going to the villa to wait for your sister. If she comes here first, tell her where I am. Don't tell her I'm mad, though. I'm saving that for a surprise."

"Are you two going to fight?"

Gray didn't have to consider it long. "Yes, we are definitely going to fight."

"Good. She's irritating."

"So are you."

"Yes, but I'm cute."

Gray's smile turned rueful. "So is she."

"You're still going to fight, though, right?"

Gray was resigned to his fate. "Yeah. We have to. It's time."

"Well, at least you have that to look forward to."

"Yes, there's always a bright side to everything."

9
NINE

Hali went straight to the bar after Andrew dropped her off. It would've been easier to go to the villa, but she figured Gray would head to the bar when he was finished with Rusty. There was just one little problem with her plan.

"What do you mean Gray has already been here and left?" Her heart sank to her shoes. "What did you tell him, Jesse?"

Being the typical little brother he was, Jesse gave her a dirty look. "I told him the truth."

"And what was the truth?"

"That you left with another man."

Hali rolled her eyes. "I don't care about that part. Gray isn't an idiot. Did you tell him who I left with?"

"I told him that you seemed upset after you got a visit from that chick, and you called the cop. Then you left with the cop."

"Crap." Hali rubbed her forehead. All around her, the night shift workers were conversing with the day shift workers as they planned to take over. "Are you trying to kill me?"

"How is this my fault?" Jesse complained. "You didn't tell me to lie."

"Siblings are supposed to stand up for each other," Hali argued.

"Oh, geez." Jesse rolled his eyes so hard it was a miracle he didn't topple over. "Maybe you should leave me with a list of lies you want me to tell next time. I thought you and Gray were all about the truthfulness."

Hali recognized being angry at her brother was stupid. She'd done this to herself. Andrew had warned her about not calling Gray. She was the one who had created this situation. It was easier to blame Jesse than herself, though. "I'm going to kick the crap out of you later."

With that, she turned on her heel and headed toward the villa. She couldn't work nights yet anyway. It was too dangerous in case she didn't see a hidden obstacle on the pavement and tripped. She'd already promised Gray she would spend at least another week on days before taking a night shift. It was the smart move.

Now, she was going to have to deal with the problem she'd wrought ... and she wasn't looking forward to it.

It only took Hali a few minutes to get to the villa. Her hip was starting to ache a bit—this was the most she'd walked on it since the surgery—and what she wanted most was her ice bag and Gray. Not even in that order. She was going to get a fight instead. She just knew it.

Wayne, her drunken flamingo familiar, was standing on the front walk when she arrived. She hadn't seen him for two days—he'd been making up for lost time since he decided to dry out for a bit—and his hangovers were stretching late into the afternoon these days.

"Is he inside?" she asked by way of greeting.

"If you're talking about your grumbly wolf, then yes, he's inside. He doesn't seem to be in the best mood."

Hali cringed. "What's he doing?"

"Laundry. Dishes. He went on a vacuuming spree."

Gray was a man who needed to be kept busy when he was agitated. The fact that he'd likely cleaned the villa from top to bottom was not surprising. "Thanks." Her feet felt heavy as she trudged toward the steps. There were only three of them, but she took care as she climbed. The pain was more than she was prepared for.

Gray was in the kitchen when she walked through the door. His back was to her. Since he had super shifter hearing, she had no doubt that he'd heard her enter the villa. He didn't look up, though.

Hali stood on the other side of the door, debating, and then took two limping steps toward the kitchen. Her plan was to grab the ice bag and then flop on the couch so Gray could rant and rave. Apparently, her uneven footsteps were enough to draw his attention, though.

"Sit down," he said when he saw she was having trouble moving.

"I'm fine," she said automatically.

"Sit down, Hali." Gray wiped his hands on a towel and tossed it on the counter before heading toward the freezer. He grabbed the now familiar blue bag and frowned when he crossed and found her still standing. "You're going to be the death of me." He carefully wrapped his arm around her waist and lifted her from the ground. He wasn't as gentle as normal when he carried her to the couch. Then he proceeded to arrange it so she was leaning against him, and he could plant the ice bag on her hip, keeping a firm pressure so the cold would seep in faster.

"You want to fight, don't you?" Hali asked.

"Yup." Gray saw no reason to lie. "I definitely want to fight."

"I figured." Hali let loose a sigh. "Do you want to hear the story first, or jump right into it?"

"Let's start with the story."

Hali swallowed hard. "Her name is Angela Brennan. She paid me a visit at the tiki bar this afternoon."

"I figured that's who you were talking to." Gray didn't say anything else. He just studied her face.

Hali felt distinctly uncomfortable having him stare down at her the way he was. She pushed forward anyway. "She offered me a deal. If I prove she's innocent of the charges that got her locked away, she won't go after you again."

Even though Gray had prepared himself for a scenario very similar to the one Hali had laid out, he was still jarred by the news. "I don't want you putting yourself at risk for me."

"You don't get a choice in the matter. I can't let her hurt you."

"Hali." Gray said her name on a growl.

"Don't even pretend you wouldn't do the same thing for me," she warned.

"Were you going to tell me about this? If I hadn't gotten to the bar early, were you even going to tell me you talked to her?"

Hali answered truthfully. "Yes. I was going to try to get you liquored up, so you were calmer and easier to distract with kisses, though."

Gray didn't want to smile. It would only encourage her. He couldn't help himself, though. "You are ... unbelievable sometimes."

"Yeah."

"Where did you and Andrew go?"

"Zephyrhills Correctional."

"You talked to her cellmate," he surmised.

Hali nodded. "She was fairly forthcoming. She was one of the escapees that got caught right away. I had to put fifty bucks in her commissary, but she basically admitted that Angela didn't make real friends and has a vendetta against her twin sister, Cammie."

"Why?"

Hali shrugged. "I'm not sure. Angela was locked up for murdering her boyfriend, who happened to live in the same building. He was a drug dealer and stabbed six times in the back. She claims she didn't do it."

"And she's saying the sister did?"

"I guess. We stopped at their mother's house on our way back. I guess the father isn't part of the picture. He took off when they were little. The mother is a mess. There was like a pound of pot on the coffee table when we were there. Andrew promised he wasn't going to arrest her for drugs if she talked.

"Basically, she said Cammie and Angela were taken from her by social workers multiple times when they were growing up," she continued. "She always got them back, except for the last time when they were teenagers."

"I'm almost afraid to hear what happened the last time they were taken," Gray murmured.

"Apparently, Laura—she's the mother—was mad at Angela at the time and told the social workers Cammie was a good girl and Angela wasn't." Hali was still mad about it. "Cammie got put in a decent home. She actually had people help her with homework and grades. Angela went to a group home, and I don't think things went as well for her.

Laura doesn't know, though, because she's too caught up in her own stuff to care about her daughters."

"Not everybody has a family that cares, Hali."

Hali jerked up her chin. "It's not the same as you, but I get why you're angry with your mother. As for Angela, I don't know what to do here. She's adamant that she didn't do it."

"And she's threatening me to get what she wants," Gray said. "She understands that I'm your weak spot. How did she figure out who you were?"

"Apparently, it wasn't that difficult. She says there are paranormal message boards, and I'm the talk of half of them."

"You are. People are in awe of you. I read those message boards right after we met. You're like a unicorn to some of these people."

Hali didn't know what to make of that. She was uncomfortable thinking on it too long. "Don't be mad at Andrew. He told me to call you. I just wanted to see if I could figure it out before I had to make you mad at me."

Gray flipped the ice bag over and pressed the cold side to Hali's hip. "I get why you did it," he said finally. "You can't protect me from everything, though."

"Now might not be the time to say it, but right back at you."

A small smile curved Gray's lips. "I know I've been smothering you a bit, and I'm sorry."

"You haven't been smothering me. It's just ... we can't spend every moment of every day together. It's not healthy. Also, even though I'm recovering, I'm still an independent person. I'm not used to having to justify my actions."

"I'm not asking you to justify them. I'm asking you to keep me in the loop."

"What would you have done if I called you?"

"Pitched a fit and guilted you to stay at the tiki bar so I could go with Andrew."

"See, I knew that." Hali made a face. "I was in a no-win position."

Gray smirked despite himself. "Perhaps you were. I'm still kind of mad."

"Are you going to pretend you're not because you want to dote on me?"

"Yup. I want to make sure your hip is okay. I was thinking we would just eat here tonight."

Hali balked. "I want to eat somewhere else. We've eaten here for almost three weeks straight."

"I don't want to drive."

"Then we'll go somewhere close on the beach. There's that Mexican place that's really good. You can even carry me. Plus, since I'm not on painkillers any longer, I can have a drink."

Gray had forgotten about the painkillers. He angled himself to look down at her. "Are you okay? Without the painkillers I mean. How much does your hip hurt?"

Hali was expecting the question. "It doesn't feel great. I didn't feel it until it was time to come home, though. It's going to be okay. Even if I feel this pain at the end of a shift every day for the rest of my life, it's still better than what it was."

Gray didn't want her in pain. More than that, though, he wanted to give her some semblance of normalcy. "Fine. We'll get tacos. You, however, will let me carry you and not complain. That's your penance."

"I just said that."

"It's more fun when I say it."

"Says you."

He grinned. "I love you, Hali Waverly. Every contrary inch of you."

She smiled back. "I love you, too, even though you're bossy."

"You're bossy too. Don't kid yourself."

"Do you want to tell me about Russell?"

"We didn't find him. We think he was in two of the locations, but not recently. We could be on the right track."

"Or it could be a wild goose chase."

"There is that, too."

"Well ... tomorrow is a new day."

"Yes, and we're going to finish this day together. We'll do twenty more minutes of this and then get dinner."

"And a cocktail." Hali was ridiculously excited about that. "I'm getting one of those huge margaritas."

"Knock yourself out. We can talk more about Angela over dinner."

Hali's smile disappeared. "She worries me. She knows I'll do whatever it takes to protect you."

Gray was worried about that, too. He didn't let her see it, though. "We'll figure it out. I won't let anything happen to you."

"I won't let anything happen to you either."

"Then I guess we're good."

He might've said the words, but he didn't feel it. He was afraid for her as much as himself. What were they going to do here?

HALI WAS HALF-BUZZED OFF A SINGLE MARGARITA when they left the Mexican place. She was a giggling and happy mess, though, which was something Gray appreciated. He carried her down the beach, until they were in front of the tiki bar, and then planted her on the sand so they could enjoy the night.

"How are you feeling?" He positioned his hands on his hips and stared down at his happy girlfriend.

She opened her arms. "Come down here, and I'll show you."

Even though Gray had been determined to hold on to some of the anger he'd been hoarding like gold as he waited for her to return to the villa, he couldn't pull it off. She was just too happy, too cute. She hadn't giggled like this in a long time. He wanted to bask in it.

"Fine." He dropped to the sand next to her and let her pull him in for a hug. Her skin was warm and soft, and he brushed his lips against her neck as he pulled her tightly against him. "How drunk are you?" he asked when he felt her hands start to wander.

"You wouldn't think I would be drunk at all," she replied. "I feel a little tipsy, though."

"You haven't had a drink in more than three weeks."

"Technically, I had a drink right before we took out the merrow."

"I actually forgot about that. Still, that drink was watered down. It wasn't even a full shot. I think there are three shots in what you drank tonight."

"And I'm feeling each and every one." Hali dissolved into giggles again when he began tickling her. She was floating on happiness, despite what was hanging over her head. There was little she loved more than a beach rendezvous with Gray.

Then she felt it. There was a creeping sensation moving over her spine. When she jerked up her head, she found Angela standing about twenty feet away. She had a woman unconscious at her feet. "Gray." Hali choked out his name.

Gray read the change in Hali's demeanor in an instant. He pulled away from her, prepared to stand as a shield, and scowled when he met Angela's amused gaze. "Stay away from her," he warned.

"Oh, look at you," Angela trilled. "You talk big for a guy I could make bark like a dog with a flick of my wrist."

"Don't even think about it." The alcohol Hali had been enjoying coursing through her system dried up in an instant. "What do you want? Who is that?" She gestured toward the unconscious woman.

"This is Joy Martelle," Angela replied. "She's a bad one. She killed her own children. I caught her trying to carjack a woman on the main highway and stopped her. Then I thought I would deliver her to you."

"And why would you want to do that?" Gray demanded.

"Because I don't like child killers and if she carjacks a woman—who had a child in the backseat of her car mind you—that's just going to increase the police presence around here."

"Ah, so it was a way to protect yourself." Gray glanced at the fallen woman. "She's not dead, is she?"

"Just knocked out," Angela replied. "For someone like Joy here, being locked up is worse than death. I don't want to give her what she wants." She focused on Hali. "Did you make any progress after our conversation this afternoon?"

"Well, we went to the prison to ask what sort of inmate you were," Hali replied.

"I was a model inmate. I'm not going back, though, so that seems like a waste of time."

"Not when we were trying to find insight on you," Hali argued. "I met your mother."

Angela stilled. "And how is Laura? I'm guessing she's still a mess."

"She is a mess. Her boyfriend Rick is a real winner, too."

"Ah, Rick." Angela cocked her head. "I'm surprised he's even still around. Most of her boyfriends flee after a couple of months. She's a lot of work."

"She is, but we were trying to figure out why you would be so interested in your twin sister given the nature of your purported crime."

Angela narrowed her eyes. "Did you find Cammie?" Her tone took on a dark and dangerous edge.

"Not yet," Hali replied. "Laura doesn't know where she is. Apparently, you guys stopped calling her and dropping by when you were teenagers."

"Do you blame us?"

"No." Hali tamped down the burst of sympathy that threatened to overwhelm her. "You guys got the raw end of the deal in the parental department. It sucks. I'm sorry you had to deal with that."

"But you still don't like me," Angela surmised.

"No, I don't. You're threatening the person I love most."

"I'm not doing that because I want to," Angela replied. "I'm doing it because I have no choice. Clear my name and you'll both be home free."

"Don't push Hali," Gray argued. "Just ... stay away from her."

"No offense, big guy—and I see why she's head over heels for you—but you don't get a say in this," Angela fired back. "There's nothing you can do to help me. I mean ... other than help your girlfriend clear my name. She's going to be the one doing the heavy lifting. This arrangement is with her."

"Stay away from her," Gray insisted.

"No. I need her." Angela turned back to Hali. "As for you, figure it out. I can only stay off the radar of the cops for a short amount of time. If you don't give me what I want, I'll have no choice but to take what you love." Her gaze was heavy when it landed on Gray. "Get to it."

Hali watched her go—she couldn't stop her because that would put Gray at risk—and then dropped her head into her hands. The happiness she'd been feeling only minutes before was gone.

"Baby, don't," Gray said as he rubbed her back. "We'll figure it out." He slowly got to his feet and approached the unconscious woman. "I guess I should call Andrew. He needs to pick up this chick—I remember reading stories about her—and we have to come up with a story about how we got her."

"Yeah." Hali pulled out her phone. "You watch her. I'll call Andrew."

"It's going to be okay, Hali," Gray promised.

Hali hoped that was true. She felt as if she was drowning, though. She had no idea where to look to help Angela, and she was running out of time. She could just feel it.

10
TEN

Andrew was annoyed when he got called out to the beach. He took one look at the prone form on the sand and then stared up at the sky, as if trying to get answers from some all-powerful deity.

"Why is it always you guys?" he complained.

"Sorry." Gray held out his hands. "We didn't nab her."

"Angela did," Hali said darkly.

"You saw her?" Andrew jerked up his chin. "What did she say?"

"The same stuff she's been saying. If I want to keep Gray safe, I have to prove she was innocent."

Andrew slowly slid his eyes to Gray. "I take it you've been caught up on this afternoon's activities."

"I have. You went out on a date with my girl. Jesse told me all about it."

Andrew made a protesting sound. "It was not a date." His eyes were wild when he turned them to Hali. "Tell him it wasn't a date."

For a moment, Hali considered messing with him. Since he looked tired—and they needed a favor from him—she didn't give in to her darker urges. "He knows. He's just screwing with you."

Andrew glared at Gray. "That's not funny."

Gray chuckled. "I have to get my jollies somewhere," he said. "I was having a grand time with my tipsy girlfriend before Angela showed up and ruined it."

Andrew hunkered down and stared at Joy. "Do you know what she did to her?"

"No, but I'm guessing she won't stay knocked out forever," Hali answered.

"Probably not." Andrew removed the cuffs from his belt. "What was she trying to do again?"

"Apparently, she was trying to carjack someone, and Angela stopped her," Gray answered. "That's what she told us anyway. I think we need to be careful when explaining this."

"We need to keep it as close to the truth as possible," Andrew agreed. "You two need to say you saw Angela on the beach with Joy and that Angela dropped her when she saw you and ran. You can't say you found Joy trying to carjack someone."

"Because we don't even know if that's true so far," Gray surmised.

"Pretty much," Andrew confirmed. "I'm sure it has been or will be reported. We can put the two stories together after the fact. All you guys saw was Angela with Joy."

"I remember the stories about Joy," Hali offered. "I was working at a bar downtown when it happened. She drove her car into the water but claimed that she'd been carjacked, right?"

Andrew nodded. "She said two Hispanic men carjacked her and the kids were in the back seat. Turns out she had a boyfriend, and he didn't want kids. The kids drowned in their car seats."

Hali felt sick to her stomach. "Well, I'm glad she's not still running around. How many are still out there?"

"Seven, including Angela," Andrew replied. "I'm hopeful one or two turn themselves in tonight now that word is spreading we won't add charges for anybody who turns themself in. We caught Barb Sinclair outside her daughter's house. She was in the bushes, still in her orange jumpsuit. We also caught Liz Duncan at the bus station. Joy makes three of the ten."

"What do you think I should do about Angela?" Hali asked. She was genuinely curious. "She seems to know she doesn't have a lot of time. If I don't come up with results, she's going to do something to show me she means business." She darted a worried look toward Gray. "Maybe ... maybe you should move away from the beach until this is over."

The look Gray shot her was withering. "I'm not leaving you."

"I know but..." Hali wasn't certain what she should say. "I'm just afraid."

"Baby, we're going to figure it out." Gray tried not to let his frustration show. "Just don't do anything weird, okay?"

Hali's lower lip came out to play.

"Okay?" he prodded.

"I think I need another drink." Hali struggled to her feet. What she really needed was to think. The tiki bar wasn't that far away. "I'll leave you guys to this." She turned and then groaned when she heard Gray hurrying to catch up with her.

"Let me carry you," he insisted in a low voice.

"I'm fine. It's not that far." Even saying it had Hali's hip twinging.

"I know you want a little space because you're upset, but putting your recovery back isn't going to help matters," Gray argued. "Just ... let me carry you."

"Or you could let me carry her," a new voice offered.

Hali and Gray swung in tandem and found Vinson Madden, a local vampire whom they were both fond of, studying them. He was near a crop of palm trees, downwind, and neither of them had noticed him lurking.

"Hey." Hali was relieved to see him. "I'm so glad you're here. I haven't seen you since ... well ... you know when."

"Since we ended the merrow." Vin moved closer. "You've been recuperating. I've been sending out feelers to make sure there aren't any merrow still around. There aren't in case you're wondering. I'll take you to the bar." He said it to Hali, but his gaze was on Gray.

"I think that's a good idea," Gray said. "She's had a rough day and could use someone to talk to who isn't me."

"Oh, don't say it like that," Hali complained. If aggrieved was a person, it would be her, Gray mused.

"Get her a drink," he said to Vin. "I'll be up there in a few minutes. I just need to help Andrew with this."

"And what is this?" Vin cocked his head as he regarded Joy. "Is that one of the prisoners?"

"Yes." Gray nodded. "Hali will fill you in."

"Then I can't wait to hear it." Vin was an old school gentleman, which meant he was beholden to manners. "May I put my arm around your waist?" he asked Hali.

Hali nodded. "You're not mad, right?" she asked Gray as Vin slid his arm around her.

"I'm not," Gray assured her. "It's been a tough day for

both of us. Get your drink. Have some water too, huh? I won't be long."

"Okay."

Gray was silent as he watched them go. As a vampire, Vin had zero issues carrying Hali. When he was certain they were out of earshot—or Hali at least—he turned back to Andrew. "I'm worried," he announced.

"Hali will be fine," Andrew replied. "She's just frustrated because she's not back at a hundred percent."

"That's not what I'm worried about," Gray countered. "I'm worried that Angela is going to swoop in and make me do something to hurt her."

"Why would she do that?" Andrew challenged. "She needs Hali to prove her innocence. Or at least that's what she's convinced herself. She can't hurt Hali and expect Hali to give her what she wants."

"She can hurt Hali in different ways."

"Give me a 'for instance.'"

"Okay, for instance, what if she were to take me over and tell me to kill Jesse?"

Dread paled Andrew's face. "I did not think that out."

"I don't have to hurt Hali directly. I can break her a million different ways, though."

"Then maybe you should follow Hali's suggestion and leave the beach until this is over."

"I can't be away from Hali. It will kill me."

"Well, that was a little dramatic." Andrew let loose a low laugh.

"I can't be away from her, and I can't bear the thought of her getting hurt," Gray said. "That means we're going to have to try to prove Angela is innocent."

"What if she's not, though?"

"We'll cross that bridge when we come to it."

Andrew nodded. "For now, I need you to help me get Joy to the front of the resort. Hali will be safe with Vin. As for the rest ... we're just going to have to figure it out as it comes along."

"Yeah. It's frustrating."

"It's totally frustrating. It is what it is, though."

"OF COURSE YOU WOULD CHOOSE THE mermaid drink." Vin wrinkled his nose as he studied the blue concoctions Hali had ordered when one of her servers came over to check on them.

"They're good," Hali replied. "I love them." To prove it, she took a long sip. She'd taken the opportunity to catch Vin up on everything that had happened during the walk up to the bar, and as they were waiting for one of the servers to wait on them. As of yet, he hadn't responded. "Tell me what to do."

"Ah, Hali, I can't tell you what to do because I don't know what you should do," Vin replied. "It's a fraught situation. The smart thing would be for Gray to remove himself from the situation."

"He's not going to do that."

"No, he won't, and you don't really want him to. You understand that it's the smart move, but you want him with you as much as he wants to be with you."

"I'll spend all my time worrying if he's not with me," Hali agreed. "What if Angela tries to make him kill one of my workers or something, though?"

"Let's just hope she doesn't."

"I have to be more proactive than that."

"Okay, what are your options?" Vin sounded utterly reasonable as he sipped his cocktail. The way he wrinkled his nose told Hali exactly what he thought of being forced into a frilly cocktail. He would never deny her, though.

"We have to find the sister." It was all Hali could come up with. "The cellmate said that Angela was obsessed with her sister to the point of distraction."

"So, you think the sister killed the boyfriend."

"Or Angela believes the sister killed the boyfriend," Hali countered. "It's possible it's somebody else entirely. I have no choice but to find Cammie, though."

"I can send out some feelers. If Angela is a witch, there's every possibility that Cammie is a witch too."

It was something Hali hadn't considered, and she wanted to kick herself for it. "I didn't ask the mother if magic ran in their family. Given her living situation, I'm going to guess the magic either skipped Laura, ran through their father, or they got involved in a coven as teenagers or something."

"The level of magic you described to me suggests this isn't found magic," Vin argued. "I would think they had to have been born with it."

"Maybe I can have Gray pull the birth certificates," Hali mused. "They should list the father. If I can track him down, I might get some answers. Or maybe even enough blood to perform a binding ritual."

Vin's eyebrows winged up. "Do you think that's possible?"

"Anything is possible. I'm going to have to get my grandmother's help, I'm sure. She'll put the whole coven on it."

"You could put your grandmother on it now," Vin suggested. "She might be able to ward the entire beach and keep Gray safe."

"Except he can't stay here forever. He's got his own stuff

going on. He and Rusty spent the entire day looking for Russell."

"He's still out there, huh?" Vin didn't look particularly surprised. "I don't think he's gone far. He can't. This is the only world he knows. I'm guessing he's trying to figure out a way to stay in power."

"That's not going to happen. They won't let it."

"No, but that won't stop him from trying. Make sure you're not so distracted with Angela that you open yourself up to attack from Russell."

"Russell isn't stupid enough to hit this beach just yet. There's no way."

"Fear makes people stupid."

"Yeah." Hali looked up as Gray crossed from the sidewalk to them. He was sweaty, but otherwise looked unharmed. "Did you get Joy into Andrew's cruiser?"

"Yes." Gray lowered himself into the chair next to Hali. "She didn't look heavy, but she was dead weight. While we were at the car, a report came in. The woman who was almost carjacked called it in. She said an angel saved her and then hauled off the carjacker."

"An angel?" Hali sipped her drink. "That won't go to Angela's head or anything."

"No, but it does prove she was telling the truth," Gray said. "Maybe she isn't evil incarnate."

"She's still dangerous." It was something Hali couldn't let go. "She's dangerous to you because she knows I love you. I'm putting you in danger."

"We are not having that fight." Gray was firm. "You've been in danger because of me. I've been in danger because of you. It's not a competition. We're a unit, and we're staying that way."

"Does that mean you're going to help me prove that Angela is innocent?" Hali was hopeful.

"I don't see where we have much choice."

She let loose the breath she didn't realize she was holding. "Thank you."

"No thanks necessary. I want us to get out of this unscathed just as much as you. So, we'll work together and see what we come up with."

"I'll send some feelers out too," Vin offered. "Angela's magic shouldn't be able to work on my kind. It's the mirror image thing. There's nothing there for her to grab onto. Maybe, if we're lucky, we can find her first and it won't be an issue."

Hali wanted to ask what the vampires would do with Angela if they caught her, but she thought better of it. "I appreciate the help."

"Anytime." Vin drained his drink. "Now, if you'll excuse me, I'm heading down the beach for a real drink. You should get some ice on that hip. No matter how much you want to pretend otherwise, you're in pain. I can tell by the way you're holding yourself."

Hali scowled at him. "Thanks. Now Gray is going to baby me all night."

"Don't pretend you don't like it." Vin winked at her. "Go home. Get some rest. I'll be in touch." With that, the darkness swallowed him.

"Finish your drink," Gray said. "Then we're going home so you can bond with your ice pack. I'll start researching once we're in bed and you're no longer in pain."

"It doesn't hurt that much," Hali hedged.

"I don't care. It's time to rest."

"Fine, but I'm only doing it because I think it's a good idea too."

"I can live with that."

ONCE HALI WAS IN HER PAJAMAS, TUCKED IN at his side with the ice pack on her hip and her head on his shoulder, Gray started searching.

"I found the birth certificates," he said. "The father is listed as unknown."

"Crap." Hali made a face. "I was hoping it would be easier than that."

"I can send Rusty over to talk to the mother again tomorrow. He can schmooze information out of anybody. She might be more willing to talk to him when she realizes he's not a cop."

"Do you think finding the father is important?"

"I think it can't possibly hurt and very well may be important."

"Then I guess that's what we have to do."

Gray brushed his lips over her forehead before he started typing again. "As for Cammie, I don't think she's going by the last name Brennan any longer. She seems to have fallen off the map."

"When?"

"Weirdly enough, it was right around the time that Seth Rochester was killed. Cammie Brennan just stopped existing."

"Don't you have to file paperwork to change your name?"

"Legally, yes. I don't think this was legal, though. I think she likely just changed her last name."

"But ... don't you need a Social Security number to be paid and stuff?"

"Again, legally. It's possible she's being paid off the books."

Hali took a moment to think about it. "She would have to be pretty scared to go that route, right? You're not going to see a lot of upward momentum in cash only jobs."

"No, you are not," Gray agreed. "She must have seen something that scared her."

"So, either she killed the boyfriend and framed her sister, or she saw someone else do it and is afraid for her life," Hali surmised. "We're going to have to make her feel safe when we find her."

"If she's a killer, she'll see us as marks," Gray countered. "Also, she might have the same abilities as her sister. We need to be careful."

"Yeah." Hali tightened her grip on Gray's arm. "We have family breakfast tomorrow. I would suggest getting out of it, but you've met my parents. It will be a big deal if we skip."

"It's okay," Gray said. "We can do family breakfast. After that, I have some contacts I can tap in Tampa to help find Cammie. I don't know if they'll be able to come through—it's a long shot—but there's no harm in trying."

"Okay." Hali angled her head so her mouth touched his stubbled cheek. "I wasn't suggesting that you go to your brother's place because I don't want you around," she said. "I need you to know that."

"I do know that. You're afraid for me. I'm afraid for me too. My fear for you outweighs my fear for myself, though."

"See, my fear for you outweighs my fear for myself."

"We're quite the pair." He slid his arm around her back and tugged her tight. "We'll be careful."

"A lot more careful than we were tonight."

"That goes without saying. Angela is a threat, but if

she's telling the truth, she's not the sort of threat that is going to try to kill us."

"I want to believe that, but I'm not sure I can," Hali admitted. "There's something about her. Something dark. Even if she was innocent when she got locked away. Prison changes people. Innocence does not equate to goodness."

"You think she's a bad person," Gray realized.

"I think she has darkness."

"Don't we all?"

"Her darkness is the type that can swallow us all."

"We won't let it. We've been up against worse than her."

"Yeah. It's going to be a battle, though."

"We can handle a battle."

Hali closed her eyes. "I won't lose. Not when the ultimate prize is you."

"That's good to hear, because I'm not going to lose either." He gave her a kiss. "Now, get some sleep. I have a feeling we're going to need our energy for tomorrow."

"I have a feeling you're right."

11
ELEVEN

Hali spent time doing her hair and makeup the next morning, something that caught Gray off guard. He smiled when she met him by the front door, but he had questions.

"Is there something I should know?" He brushed a flyaway strand of hair away from her face.

"What do you mean?" Confusion lined Hali's features. "What's wrong?"

"Well ... are you getting all gussied up for somebody specific?"

Hali made a face. "First off, who uses the word 'gussied' in this day and age?"

"I heard your grandmother use it the other day when she was talking to Rusty."

Hali's smile grew tight. "You saw my grandmother and Rusty?"

Gray nodded. "They're still hanging out."

Hali didn't want to make a big deal out of it—her grandmother fed off of disapproval—but the amount of time Gray's brother was spending with her grandmother made her uneasy. There was a lot of flirting going on. True, it could've been harmless flirting. Still, Hali was bothered.

"I can't take it if Rusty becomes my step-grandfather," she warned Gray.

He laughed. "I'm fairly certain they're just doing it for attention."

"What if they're not, though?"

He shrugged. "They're consenting adults."

"Oh, do you know something?"

"I know my girl got all dressed up."

Hali glanced down at her linen shorts and simple top. "This is not dressed up."

"Lately it is."

"That's why I did it. My mother mentioned on the phone the other day that she's afraid I'm getting too complacent in our relationship. She says men don't like knit shorts and no bra."

Gray chuckled. He enjoyed Hali's parents. Actually, he found the entire family hilarious. Her mother, Joyce, had a few antiquated thoughts on relationships, though. She was intent that Hali learn how to cook so she could keep Gray happy with food. He'd told Hali it was nonsense—he was perfectly happy eating takeout the rest of his life—but Joyce kept trying to force Hali into cooking classes.

He found the whole thing delightful.

This, though, was different. "Baby, here's a little-known tip. Men are fine when the women they love don't wear bras."

Hali snorted. "And no makeup?"

"I think you're the most beautiful woman in the world whether you're wearing makeup or not."

"I went a full week without running a brush through my hair after my surgery," she reminded him.

"Yes, but you let me help you shower so you didn't smell." His smile was soft. "That stuff is never going to be a factor for me, Hali. Don't let your mother get you worked up."

"Maybe I want to get dressed up," she challenged. "Have you ever considered that?"

"I happen to know you're happiest in your knit shorts. And who needs a bra?"

Hali giggled, making the sound he loved above all else. She slid in front of him as he opened the door. "I'll keep that in mind. You should probably not mention that in front of my father, though."

"I'm not an idiot."

She paused. "Thank you for everything." She was earnest as she met his gaze.

Confused, Gray tilted his head. "What are you thanking me for?"

"You took care of me. You didn't have to."

"Hali, I always want to take care of you."

"You don't understand how rare that is."

"Well, you'd better get used to it. You're not getting rid of me."

"I guess it's good I kind of like you, huh?"

"I think it's definitely good."

GRAY PARKED IN FRONT OF HALI'S PARENTS' house and hurried around to the passenger door so he could help Hali. She was getting stronger each and every day, but he didn't want her to accidentally slip on a curb or something. If her recovery was set back for such a mundane reason, they would both grow frustrated.

"Okay?" he asked once she was steady on the sidewalk.

"I'm good," she promised. She meant it. "Don't worry about me."

"It goes with the territory." He held her hand for the walk to the front door. He knocked because he felt he should, but Hali made a face and opened the door.

"We don't knock here," she complained as she walked into the living room.

"They knock at our place," he pointed out.

"They never come to our place."

"They've knocked the two times they've visited," he argued.

"Yes, but we're naked in our place a lot more than they're naked here."

"Or maybe you just wish that."

Hali glared at him. "Don't freak me out. I mean ... my brother still lives here. If they're playing naked games, then that's a level of kink that is going to freak me out forever."

Sensing a set of eyes on him, Gray raised his chin, and found Steve Waverly watching him. Hali's father loved his children beyond measure. He was actually fond of Gray, too. That didn't mean he was okay watching the sexual innuendo fly between his middle child and the man who had taken over her life in such a short amount of time.

"Hello, sir," Gray said in a boisterous voice. He held out his hand to shake. "How are you?"

Steve glanced at Gray's hand, then over at his daughter. "You have a voice that carries, Hali," he complained.

"You have three children," Hali replied, unruffled by her father's tone. "You know about being naked. Don't give me grief."

Steve made a face, then motioned for them to follow him into the kitchen. "We're still cooking. You can sit while we finish it up."

"I'm much better," Hali assured her father. "You don't have to worry about me."

"I'm your father. I'm going to worry about you for the rest of your life. That's how it works."

"I can help," Gray offered when they reached the kitchen. He nudged Hali toward a chair, even though she sent him a death glare. "Hali should rest."

"Don't push me," Hali warned. "I don't need to rest. I'm better."

"You *are* better," Gray agreed. "You still need to rest so you keep getting better."

"How are you feeling?" Joyce asked. She had pancake batter on her face and looked to be elbow deep in preparations when Gray crossed to help her. "You should stay with Hali," she argued. "I think you've been putting in long hours with her. You deserve a bit of a break, too."

"I like to help," Gray replied.

Joyce smirked. "It's okay to take a break. I know Hali is a lot."

"I'm right here," Hali complained.

"We could never miss you," Steve said. He seemed happy to slip in and help his wife as Gray sat next to Hali at the table, which was already set. "Seriously, Hali, how are you feeling? It's been a few weeks now."

Hali understood why her parents were worried. She'd been worried about the same thing, to the point where she'd turned into something of a monster for the initial stretch around her surgery. She was better now.

Well, she hoped she was better.

"I'm okay," Hali assured them as her sister, Annie, let herself in through the back door. "I still get tired. I'm going to have to work up my stamina, but I don't have the same pain I had before."

"Do you have any pain?" Steve asked.

Hali darted a look toward Gray, uncertain.

"Don't lie, Hali," Gray admonished her. "He's your father. Of course he doesn't want his child to be in pain."

"If I overextend myself, I feel sore," Hali replied. "It's not the same pain as before. It's like when you go to the gym and work out too hard. It's not the sort of pain that debilitates you."

"I guess that's good." Steve leaned in and kissed Annie's cheek, but he kept his gaze on Hali. "I don't want you in pain. What does the doctor say?"

"I had my initial checkup right after the surgery, but I don't have my next checkup for another week," Hali replied. "The doctor was happy with my first checkup. Hopefully, he'll be happy with my second."

"And you are kind of sidestepping the issue," Steve groused. He focused on Gray. "After saying kinky stuff about my daughter in my home, I think you owe me."

"That was nowhere near as kinky as we can get," Hali warned.

Gray chuckled. He was loyal to Hali to a fault, but he knew better than ignoring Steve's questions. "He's happy so far. We won't really know what Hali's new normal is until she has a bit more recuperation time. He said six weeks was the mark where we would know."

"So, that's still a few weeks away." Steve didn't look happy. "You're doing everything the doctor tells you to do, right?"

"I am being a perfect patient," Hali assured him.

Steve didn't look convinced. "Is she?" he asked Gray.

"She's being pretty good," Gray confirmed. "She went on an adventure with another man yesterday—I would've preferred she not do that—but otherwise she's being a model patient."

Hali glared at him. "Oh, I can't believe you just went there. That is low."

"You went out with another man?" Joyce looked scandalized. "Hali, what is the matter with you? You have a man who loves you right here. Why would you hurt him?"

Gray snorted when Hali lightly slapped his arm. "See. You have the perfect man already. Your mother agrees you shouldn't be going out with other men."

"You're in big trouble." Despite her desire to be annoyed, Hali couldn't stop herself from smiling. "I didn't go out with another man," she explained to her parents. "I went to Zephyrhills Correctional with a mutual friend. It was a witch thing."

Joyce had witch in her genes but never embraced the lifestyle. She understood the basics, though. "Does this have something to do with the prison break on the beach the other night?"

"You heard about that?" Hali asked.

"Everybody heard," Steve replied. "I didn't think to call you to make sure everything was okay because you've been sticking close to home of late."

"Well, ironically, that was our first night out since the surgery," Hali said. "We went to one of the restaurants on the beach and had crab legs. We were right there when the prisoners made a break for it."

"No way." Annie paused by the refrigerator door, a carton of juice in her hand. "Did you see any of them?"

"Unfortunately, we saw a few," Hali replied. "It mostly wasn't a big deal until one of them cast a spell on Gray."

Gray stiffened but kept his expression neutral.

"You were under a spell?" Annie's eyes widened. Unlike

her sister, she didn't have access to magic. It seemed to have completely skipped her.

"It wasn't my finest moment," Gray replied. "In fact, I don't like thinking about it too much. Things could've gone terribly wrong for Hali."

"They didn't, though." Hali shot him a quelling look. "Don't you start."

Gray poked her side, amused despite himself. "Then you'd better not start." He exhaled heavily when he realized all of Hali's relatives—sans Jesse, who apparently wasn't up yet—were watching him. "It was a horrible event. I'm not happy. We're trying not to fixate on it, though, because we'll go crazy."

"What's the plan?" Joyce asked. "How are you going to make sure it doesn't happen again?"

"Well, there's one way." Because she didn't have a choice, Hali told her parents everything. She explained about Angela, and how she was determined to clear her name. She told them about visiting Angela's cellmate and mother. When she was finished, her parents and sister all started talking at once.

"Do you think she's going to try to kill Gray?" Joyce asked.

"Maybe Gray shouldn't be staying with you right now," Steve suggested. "I can come over and stay with you. That way you won't have to worry."

"I know Cammie," Annie volunteered out of the blue.

Hali's jaw swung in the breeze as she decided who to respond to first. "I don't think killing Gray will get her what she wants," she said to her mother finally. "She will try to use him to force my hand, though."

"Well, that's not nice." Joyce made a sniffing noise. "I hope she gets arrested soon."

"Thanks, Mom." Hali unleashed a bland smile. "As for Gray and I separating, we have talked about that. Neither one of us is willing to be away from the other."

"Some people might call that codependent," Steve noted.

"Yes, well, it is a little codependent," Hali agreed. "You coming to stay with me would be no different than Gray staying with me, though. Angela could simply force you to do her bidding, leaving me to try to stop you instead of him."

"I guess I didn't think about that." Steve was rueful. "Still, I don't like this. I think you two should be careful."

"Maybe Gray can stay here," Annie suggested. "That way you can spy on him to your heart's content."

"Don't push me, young lady," Steve warned. "I'm not in the mood for your crap."

Annie didn't look bothered when she turned back to Hali. "Did you hear what I said?"

"I did," Hali confirmed. "You said the most interesting thing."

"I happen to believe I said the most interesting thing," Steve argued.

Hali ignored him. "You said you know Cammie? How?"

"Well, I know a Cammie Brennan. She goes by a different last name now, though."

Hali glanced at Gray and found him following the conversation with rapt attention. "And what name is that?"

"Cammie Bryson."

"How do you know her?" Gray asked. He was already typing the name into his search database.

"She works at that rehabilitation center over on East Wilder. I think I've mentioned it before. It's in-house, and they're one of my biggest clients now because that business sees high turnover. When I first met her, she said her name was Cammie Bryson. A few weeks ago, though, I heard her arguing with someone on the phone. I guess she didn't make the name change legal. She asked me if I knew anything about making it official."

"What did she ask specifically?" Hali asked as Gray continued to type.

"She wanted to know if her name change had to be public," Annie replied. "She acted as if she was worried about somebody finding her. I figured, given the fact that she was working in a rehabilitation center, it was likely she had drug problems of her own in her past. It would make sense to want to hide from some of those people."

"It would," Hali agreed. She leaned to read over Gray's shoulder. "Anything?"

"I found a photo of Cammie Bryson," Gray replied. His expression was hard to read. "She's kind of in the back of a group photo." He held up his phone.

Annie edged over to look. "That's her," she confirmed. "That's the group at the rehabilitation center in fact."

Hali narrowed her eyes as she studied the image. It was a little fuzzy. "That looks like Angela."

"That's Cammie, though," Annie argued.

"They're twins," Gray volunteered. "Identical twins."

"Angela looks a little rougher around the edges, but that makes sense," Hali said. "I'm sure prison is rough on your skin."

"I'm sure you're right," Gray confirmed. He went back to working on his phone. "There's not much on her. I bet she could get paid in cash at a rehabilitation center too."

"Not necessarily," Annie argued. "Most of those places are funded through government grants. It's not just private funds for patients. Government grants mean you have to jump through a lot of hoops."

"For part-time employees too?"

"I ... huh." Annie cocked her head. "That's actually an interesting question. I bet they only have to report all of their full-time employees, because otherwise it would be a lot of paperwork that nobody wants to read."

"Which means Cammie could work thirty-nine hours a week, off the books, and be paid with cash," Gray said. "If she had a sob story about hiding from someone and fearing for her life, I can see that flying in a place like that. When was the last time you saw her?" he asked Annie.

"Um ... about two weeks ago." Annie looked puzzled. "Why is that important?"

"Because Angela is adamant that Cammie did something to her, and now Angela has very publicly escaped from prison," Gray said. "My guess is that Cammie isn't feeling all that joyful right now."

"You think she ran," Annie realized.

"I think it's a possibility," Gray cautioned. "It's also possible she believes Angela won't be able to find her."

"So, what are you going to do?" Joyce asked. "You can't purposely turn her over to her sister."

"That's not the plan," Gray assured her. "We do need to talk to her, though." He locked gazes with Hali. "I think, after breakfast, we should take a trip over there. It can't possibly hurt to talk to Cammie."

"What if she runs?" Hali asked. "What if she really is trying to make herself a better person and we ruin her life?"

"That's not what I want," Gray replied. "However, what if the opposite is true? What if Cammie is the one who did the killing and Angela went down for it? What if Cammie is a bad person?"

"I've talked to Cammie a bunch of times," Annie argued. "She's a good person. I would know if she wasn't."

"Well, then we'll talk to her and offer whatever help we can," Gray said. "We can't do nothing. Angela is too dangerous. The police will catch up with her sooner or later. She can do a lot of damage before they take her down, though."

"Just make sure you don't expose Cammie," Annie insisted. "She's a good person. I don't want her getting hurt if you can help it."

"We'll do our best to protect Cammie. You have my word." Gray slid his arm behind Hali. "We just need some answers. I think she's the best one to provide them."

Hali didn't disagree. In fact, she was excited. Maybe they were finally getting somewhere.

12
TWELVE

The Sunset Peaks Clinic was pretty basic as far as Hali could tell. It looked to have been an office building at one time, one of those nondescript fronts that housed a real estate office next to an insurance agency and across from a temp agency. The space had all been co-opted for the clinic now, and Hali was hoping the inside was more welcoming than the outside.

"We need to be nonthreatening," Gray warned as they walked toward the front entrance. He automatically wrapped an arm around Hali's waist and lifted her on the curb without prompting. He was used to looking for hidden dangers now and didn't put a lot of thought into it. "Let's feel her out before we start grilling her."

Hali nodded. "Yeah. We don't want to freak her out. If she runs, we might never find her again."

"She's going to be ill at ease no matter what," Gray cautioned. "See if you can get a feel for her magic. If Angela has it, I have to think that Cammie has it too."

"That would be my guess." Hali ducked under Gray's

arm when he held open the door for her. "To be fair, though, I have magic, and Annie doesn't."

"I feel Annie wouldn't want to be magical," Gray replied. "She seems perfectly happy going to her nine-to-five job. She'll be happy with a husband who has a nine-to-five job and two-point-five kids. That's who she is, and there's nothing wrong with that."

"You're right," Hali confirmed. "She would be happy with that. I like a little spice with my man, though." She poked his side and elicited a grin.

"I'm your cinnamon stick of love."

Hali frowned. "You just took it to a weird place."

"I knew it as soon as I said it."

"Do you regret it?"

"No. I *am* your cinnamon stick of love."

Hali's giggle erupted hard and fast. "I guess I can live with that."

They both wiped the smiles off their faces as they approached the front desk. Gray took the lead.

"Hello." He greeted the woman sitting behind the desk, who looked to be texting away like mad on her phone, with a charming head tilt. "We're looking for Cammie Bryson."

The woman looked up. Her name tag read "Carly", and she didn't seem all that interested in dealing with potential clients until she got a look at Gray. "Hey," she sputtered out, immediately dropping her phone. "Are you looking for a counselor?"

"We have some specific issues to discuss, and were referred to Cammie," Gray replied calmly. "I would rather not speak any more about that out in the open."

"Of course." Carly was solemn as she darted her eyes toward Hali. "It's terrible when a loved one—maybe a sister—has issues that need to be attended to."

Hali had to bite the inside of her cheek to refrain from saying something snarky.

"Have a seat." Carly pointed toward the sitting area in the corner. "I'll see if Cammie is available."

"Thank you." Gray gave her a wink before moving to one of the uncomfortable chairs. "Make sure you don't sit on my lap," he chided Hali. "She'll think we're freaky siblings."

"Why does she naturally assume I'm your sister?" Hali complained. "We don't look alike."

"We both have dark hair."

"So? That doesn't mean we're siblings."

"You don't look like Annie. You resemble your mother more—as does Jesse—and Annie favors your father."

"I'm just saying that she made that assumption because she wants to jump your bones," Hali complained. "It's kind of insulting. She didn't even consider the fact that we could be together."

"She considered it," Gray countered. "She just prefers that you be my sister."

"Because she wants to jump your bones."

"I adore you." Gray beamed at her. "You are literally my favorite person in the world."

Hali didn't want to soften her stance, but she couldn't help herself. "I'm fond of you too." She couldn't stop herself from being snarky despite her best efforts. "Just as a sister, though."

"That's going to make what I have planned for you later very weird."

Hali shrugged. "It is what it is."

Carly told them they could go back five minutes later. Her eyes were dreamy as she watched Gray pass. "Good luck. I hope things work out. After the first week, you can visit your sister as often as you want. In fact, we encourage it."

Gray gave Hali's shoulder a light tap. "Won't that be fun?"

"Don't push it," Hali fired back. "I can only take so much."

"You know, I figured that was likely a step too far. I can't seem to stop myself from crossing the line."

"That's the Rusty in you."

"That's the Helene in me." Gray's expression darkened. "I don't like to think about it, though."

"You're not your mother."

"I know. I'm just ... so mad."

Hali squeezed his hand. "It's okay to be mad. Just don't make any decisions until you're not mad any longer."

"What if I'm always mad?"

Hali didn't consider it long. "Then it is what it is."

Cammie's door was open, but Gray knocked all the same. The woman behind the desk looked a lot like Angela, but there were differences. Cammie's hair was shorter. She'd had it colored so it was darker, which actually made her features pop. She didn't look as worn as Angela either.

"Hello." Her voice was soft and bright. "I understand you have a situation you would like to talk to me about." Her gaze fell on Hali, and there was confusion there. "Please come in and shut the door."

Hali sat first. Gray shut the door as instructed—it would be better for them if nobody was listening—and then sat in the chair next to Hali.

"I understand your sister has some issues." Cammie's smile was welcoming as she pointed it at Hali. "I guess we'll start with the basics. What's your drug of choice?" She cocked her head and looked Hali up and down. "Meth?"

Hali's expression twisted. "Did you seriously just ask me that? Do I look like a meth head?" she demanded of Gray.

Gray reached over and patted her knee to soothe her. "I believe there's been a misunderstanding. I didn't tell the lovely woman at the front desk that Hali was my sister. Nor did I tell her we were here for Hali. There might've been a few erroneous assumptions."

"I see." A small smile played at the corners of Cammie's mouth. "You're extremely diplomatic. I think I can ascertain what happened, though. You're a very attractive man, and Carly seems drawn to attractive men. You're not the first person who has told me she jumped to conclusions. I'll talk to her."

"That's probably wise." Gray leaned back in his chair.

"I'm sorry I assumed meth," Cammie offered to Hali. "You don't look like our normal patient or anything, but I wanted to get the conversation rolling."

"We're not actually here to get somebody accepted to your program," Gray hedged. He didn't want Cammie to feel attacked, but they were boxed into a corner, and he had to get them out of it. "We're here about Angela."

Cammie froze, her hand halfway to her glass of water. "Who?" she asked after several seconds of silence.

Hali felt a wave of pity for the woman. "We don't mean to ambush you," she assured Cammie. "It's just ... I've had the pleasure of interacting with your sister twice over the past forty-eight hours or so."

Cammie darted her eyes around, as if she expected Angela to jump out from behind a fake potted plant at any moment. "Did she send you here?"

"Not like you're assuming," Gray replied. "She has ... made her presence known, however."

"I don't want anything to do with her." Cammie was no longer amiable. She looked like a woman on the verge of panic. "How did you even find me?"

"That was a stroke of luck," Gray replied. "I don't think your sister will have the same luck. We have questions, though."

"I don't want anything to do with her," Cammie seethed. "There's a reason I changed my name. I'm trying to help people here."

"And I understand that." Gray used his most reasonable tone. "I'm not trying to out you. Your sister, however, is making threats."

"How do you even know Angela?"

"Well, Hali and I had the bad luck of being on the beach the night it was swarmed by the prisoners," Gray replied. He chose his words carefully. "We were leaving one of the restaurants when it happened. Your sister showed an interesting skill set."

Cammie's forehead creased. "You're trying really hard to say something without actually saying it."

"I am," Gray agreed. "I don't want you to think I'm crazy."

"I already think you're crazy for approaching me in this manner. You have nothing to lose."

Hali was the one who took control of the situation. "Your sister is a witch."

Cammie's eyebrows practically flew off her forehead. "Is that so?"

"You already knew that, though," Hali said. "I can feel the power inside of you. It's coiled, but there. You're a witch too. There's no point in denying it."

"Well, since you're a witch, why would I bother denying it?" Cammie leaned back in her chair. She wasn't nearly as meek as she had been when they entered her office. Hali recognized it as a defense mechanism. Cammie was going to come out swinging, whether Gray and Hali were enemies or not.

"Your sister used magic to control Gray," Hali replied. They were beyond the point of playing games. "She sent him after me because I was helping the police catch the other escapees. I managed to stop him without hurting him —too badly at least—but she has now decided that she wants me to prove her innocence. To get me to comply, she's threatening to come after Gray again."

Cammie ran her tongue over her teeth, seemingly debating. "That sounds like something she would do," she said finally, slumping in her chair. "She's never been one to use her magic responsibly."

"And I'm guessing you have," Gray said.

"I was never as interested in the magic as her," Cammie replied. "I mean ... we could both do things as children. We thought we manifested it because our mother isn't magical and it was somehow a reward or something."

Gray nodded as he scratched his cheek. "I've heard about your mother. She's ... interesting."

"In the grand scheme of things, my mother is harmless," Cammie replied. "She never sets out to hurt anybody. That's not who she is. She's also limited. She should never have been a mother."

"Where did your magic come from?" Hali asked. "Mine came from my grandmother. Nobody else in my immediate family has any abilities."

"I'm honestly not sure where it came from," Cammie replied. "We never knew our father. It could've come from his side of the family. I tried to track him down at one point, but the man I found was a magical void. He was also a drunk and living on the streets."

"You don't have a father listed on your birth certificate," Gray noted. "We looked because we thought your father might be helpful when dealing with Angela."

"My mother gave me a name a few years ago," Cammie explained. "I have no idea if that man was really our father. He didn't even remember our mother. I tried to help him—he was in the throes of alcoholism—but you can't help someone who doesn't want to be helped. That's true for my mother ... and my sister."

"Is that how you got into this business?" Gray asked.

"Actually, I kind of fell into this. It's hard to find a job when you can't use your Social Security number. This was one of the few things I could find. Turns out, I have a knack for it ... and I enjoy it. There's pleasure to be found in helping people."

"What about the ones you can't help?"

"I thought that would be depressing," Cammie acknowledged. "It turns out it's been helpful for me because I was struggling to cut ties with those who can't be helped."

"Like your mother?"

"And my sister." Cammie rested her palms on the desk. "What does my sister want with you? I'm not saying I can help—I probably can't—but it's always interesting to hear what she's up to."

"She wants us to prove that she's innocent," Hali supplied. "She seems resigned to the fact that she's going to be caught again—I don't think she's traveling too far from St. Pete Beach because she checked in on us the following day—but she wants us to prove she's innocent before that happens."

"Really?" Bafflement ran roughshod over Cammie's features. "Why would she think you can do that?"

"Just off the top of my head, I'm guessing it's because Hali and I have solved several high-profile cases in the past few months," Gray replied. "I'm a private detective by trade. I have ties to the paranormal world. And Hali, well, she's a powerful witch. Everybody in St. Pete knows who she is."

"Is that so?" Cammie studied Hali with fresh eyes. "I apologize, but I've never heard of you. To be fair, I don't spend a lot of time hanging around with other paranormals. I try to keep myself away from that world. It leads to nothing but trouble."

"You didn't want to visit your sister in prison?" Gray asked.

"Not really. Angela and I were close as children. Our final separation as teenagers, though, essentially changed the trajectory of our relationship forever."

"Because you went to a good home and your mother made sure that your sister got the worst placement imaginable," Gray surmised.

"My mother thought that Angela deserved a reality check, which is just nonsense," Cammie replied. "It's true, though. I lucked out in my final placement. I'm still in touch with the family that took me in. I have dinner with them at least once a month. Angela said she didn't blame me for how things turned out, but it was obvious that she felt resentment.

"As adults, we saw each other from time to time," she continued. "My life wasn't perfect. It took me a long time to find my place in this world. Angela, however, always seemed to be looking for trouble. That was the one thing I wanted to avoid."

"When was the last time you saw her?" Hali asked.

"Right before she was convicted. I went to her trial for a few days. I thought maybe I could help. She just started ranting and raving about how I was to blame for everything bad that ever happened to her. She kept talking about me being the good twin and her being the evil twin. She said we got put in boxes, and she could never break down the walls to her box."

"I can see how it might have felt that way," Hali said. "She can't blame you for everything simply because you got a more favorable placement than she did."

"You wouldn't think," Cammie agreed. "Bitterness is a terrible beast, though." She was quiet a beat. "I don't know what I can tell you that will help your cause. I don't want to see my sister again. She'll bring nothing but trouble to this place."

"And that's the last thing we want," Gray assured Cammie. "We just need somewhere to look. Angela is insisting she's innocent. I don't know that I believe her, but she did nab one of the other prisoners—a notorious child killer—and delivered her to us. She stopped her from carjacking a woman who had a child in her car."

"That's been proven?" Cammie queried.

"Yes. Joy Martelle."

"I remember her." Cammie's nose wrinkled. "I heard she'd been caught last night. I had no idea Angela was part of it."

"I think they're keeping that part quiet for obvious reasons," Gray said. "If Angela is innocent, I feel we should do our part to prove it. I just don't know where we should be looking."

"Angela and I were not close during the time she was dating Seth," Cammie volunteered. "I know very little about him ... and what I do know is bad. He ran with a rough crowd. Anybody could've killed him."

"Do you know anybody who was close with your sister during that time?" Hali asked. "Perhaps they could help point us toward a potential suspect."

"She had a roommate," Cammie replied. "I'm not sure how close they were, but they lived together for two years."

Gray leaned forward on his chair. "That's a good potential lead. Who is it?"

"Her name was Regina Bosley. I only met her a handful of times. She smoked a little pot, and she liked to party at area bars, but she didn't seem like a total druggie or anything. I don't know what happened to her. They wanted her to testify on Angela's behalf, but she disappeared before she could."

"Meaning she could be dead," Gray surmised.

"Maybe, or maybe she did what I did and changed her name. It wasn't that hard."

"Do you know anything about Regina?" Gray asked. "Like ... did she frequent a specific bar?"

"Actually, there's a dive bar out near you guys. It's got a terrible reputation."

"MacNasty's?" Gray prodded.

Cammie snapped her fingers. "Yes. How did you know that?"

"Because that bar is nothing but trouble. If you ever want to amuse yourself for an hour, read the Google reviews. They're hilarious."

Cammie smirked. "Regina liked to hang out there. I know she worked there for a time, too. I think the odds are long that she's still there if her goal was to disappear. It's all I've got, though. I'm sorry."

"No, we appreciate your time." Gray stood and shook

her hand. "You don't have to worry about us telling your sister where you are. You're doing good work here. We don't want to ruin that for you."

"I appreciate that." Cammie turned her gaze to Hali. "Sorry about the meth thing."

Hali merely shrugged. "I've been called worse."

"Be careful," she cautioned. "Angela will go after you hard if she decides you're the only way to get what she wants."

"Well, I'll go at her just as hard to protect what I love. I'm not afraid of her."

"You should be. She's vindictive."

"So am I." Hali slid her hand into Gray's as they headed for the door. "Keep doing what you're doing. I think you're making a difference here."

"That is the hope."

"No, that's your reality. Embrace it."

13
THIRTEEN

Their next stop was Gray's office. It was in Tampa, and they needed a computer to work on because Gray couldn't hit all of his favorite search engines on his phone. Hali was immediately taken aback when they walked into the small office—the lights were muted, soft music was playing—and she beamed at the woman behind the desk.

Joan Patton had been Gray's office manager for years. She was something of a surrogate mother to Gray—although he claimed he didn't need one—and she was the one who talked him through some of his harder decisions over the years.

Including the ones that involved his girlfriend.

Gray had been determined to avoid a romantic entanglement when he first crossed paths with Hali. In hindsight, he recognized that was fruitless. At the time, though, he hadn't wanted to open his heart to her. Loving her had been inevitable, though. He knew that now. Back then, he needed someone to talk to about his feelings. Someone who wouldn't laugh like Rusty. That someone had been Joan.

"Well, well, well." Joan's smile spread across her face. "It's about time. I can't believe I'm just meeting you now."

"How do you even know who she is?" Gray demanded. He wasn't opposed to introducing Hali and Joan—although he was a little worried his office manager would embarrass him—but he had never seen Joan get to her feet so fast.

"Please." Joan made a face. "You have three pictures of her on your desk, and I googled her when you first started mentioning her. I know exactly what she looks like." Joan crossed from behind the desk and gave Hali an effusive hug. "I'm so happy to meet you."

Hali returned the hug. Unlike Helene, who had been cold to Hali upon first meeting her, Joan couldn't have been warmer. "I'm happy to meet you, too." Hali's smile was goofy when she pulled back. "I've heard a lot about you."

"I bet it's nothing compared to what I've heard about you." Joan motioned toward the chairs at the front of her desk. "Sit down. How is your hip?"

"It's okay," Hali replied. "I fatigue pretty easily still. Gray likes to carry me around as if he's a superhero."

"That sounds like him," Joan confirmed.

Gray scowled at them as he headed for his office. "Don't mind me," he said. "I'm just going to get some actual work done."

"Speaking of that, we need to talk," Joan called to his back. "You have a couple of months left on your lease for the space, but we just got notice they're going to double the rent. I think it's time to let this place go."

Gray's face appeared in the doorway he'd just disappeared through. "Are you serious?"

Joan nodded. "You've been talking about shutting down the office and just working remotely. I don't see where we need the office any longer."

"But ... how will I see you?" Gray looked mournful.

Joan chuckled. "Well, I figured I could work remotely—it's just as easy to do intakes at coffee shops as it is to do them here—and then I can arrange to come over to you once a week or so. We're not seeing each other more than that as it is."

"I guess we're not." Gray's expression was sad. "It's the end of an era, though."

"It's just the shifting of an era," Joan countered. "You're never here. You take almost all your meetings out there now. This space is a waste of money."

"I know. I used to come here a lot." Gray glanced at Hali. "I don't suppose you can use your pull with Franklin to get me an office at Paradise Lodge, can you?"

Hali had no idea if he was serious. She had an emphatic answer, though. "Of course I can. You've stepped up to help Franklin more times than I can count."

"Not because I actually wanted to help him."

Hali firmly shook her head. "It doesn't matter. I can get you an office. Joan can even work out of it a couple of days a week if she wants. Then you can see her as much as you want." Her eyes sparkled. "And Joan and I can have coffee ... and she can come to the tiki bar for afternoon break cocktails ... and she can tell me all the stories she has on you."

Hali was a little too enthusiastic for Gray's liking. "You're way too excited for this." Despite his reticence, Gray grinned. "Wasting money on the office now feels like a dumb move. I'm selling my condo too. I practically live with you anyway."

"I already told you I'm fine with you living with me," Hali said. "We both agreed it was a great way to save up for an eventual house because real estate is so expensive in St. Pete."

"Forget real estate," Gray said. "We have to cover flood insurance."

"That too." Hali rubbed her hands together. "So, we're going to do it?"

"Just out of curiosity, how is it that you think you can get Franklin Craven to do what you want?" Joan asked. "He doesn't have that reputation."

"He doesn't," Hali agreed. "He owes me, though, and Cecily is the one who is actually in control."

"And who is Cecily?"

"His righthand woman," Gray replied. "She's a pain in the ass but pretty cool. If Hali goes to Cecily and tells her what she wants, Cecily will make it happen. Franklin won't even have a say in it."

"That sounds kind of fun." Joan patted Hali's hand. "It will be nice to be out at the beach. Plus, I'll be able to see Gray with you. I knew he'd fallen hard, but not being able to see it was practically torture."

"Well, ask me whatever you want." Hali got comfortable.

Gray stared at her a moment, marveling at the way his chest felt as if it was expanding, and then headed into his office. "Don't mind me," he called out. "I'm going to run the searches and get some actual work done."

"So you've already said. Have fun," Hali replied. "Although, when you come back, bring whatever photos you have on your desk. I want to make sure I'm cute enough in them."

"Don't I get to decide what photos you're cute in when they're on my desk?"

Joan and Hali laughed in unison.

"He knows nothing about women," Joan explained. "I

had to teach him everything he knows and it's still next to nothing."

"He's a work in progress," Hali replied. "Thankfully, he's adorable, so I don't get too agitated when he falls behind."

"Yes, he's definitely got that going for him," Joan agreed.

"You guys know I can hear you, right?" Gray barked.

"He gets so worked up," Joan lamented. "He's wound just a little too tight."

"We're working on that, too," Hali said.

"Good to know."

GRAY FOUND A DECENT AMOUNT OF INFORMATION on Regina Bosley. Like Cammie, however, she'd basically fallen off the map several years before. Right around the time Angela was going on trial for murder.

"I found her," Gray announced as he emerged from his office an hour after they'd arrived. Hali and Joan had settled in and were drinking tea when he found them exactly where he'd left them. "You guys look cozy."

"Did you really dress up like a stripper for Halloween two years ago?" Hali demanded.

Gray scowled. "Stop telling her things like that," he ordered Joan. "I wasn't a stripper really," he replied to Hali. "I was more of a pimp with an attitude."

"He was a stripper," Joan replied. "He had girls hanging all over him. He was undercover for a case, and it backfired spectacularly."

"I'm going to need to see this costume," Hali said to him.

"You see that costume every night when we go to bed," Gray fired back.

"You don't dance."

"Well, once this is over, see how drunk you can get me."

"Challenge accepted." Hali looked far too smug for Gray's liking.

"Did you hear what I said?" Gray challenged. "I found her. She goes by Regina Baxter now. She works at a little cafe only a few miles from Paradise Lodge."

"So, she changed her name, too," Hali mused. "I wonder why."

"Maybe, just like Cammie, she wanted a fresh start."

"Or they're both hiding from something specific."

"Like Angela?"

Hali nodded. "I don't want to say it because that makes our job all the more difficult, but it's entirely possible that Angela is guilty, and she just wants us to find someone to scapegoat for her."

"I've wondered that myself," Gray admitted. "I don't think we have a choice but to try, though."

"Yeah." Hali pushed herself to a standing position. "If we're going to head back, we should get going now. The traffic will be murder if we wait too long."

"Say goodbye to your new friend," Gray teased. "I'm sure you guys will be seeing more of each other before it's all said and done."

"Goodbye." Hali hugged Joan. "I'll be in touch now that I have your number. I don't think I'm going to be able to talk to Cecily today, but I promise to do it in the next few days."

"Focus on the witch," Joan said. "We have a bit of time before we have to move the office. The witch takes precedence."

"You two exchanged numbers?" Gray cocked his head, unsure. "Why?"

"Because we want to gossip about you of course," Hali replied. "Did you take that photo down like I told you?"

"No, because I don't care what you say. You're adorable in that photo."

"Fine. I'll just pick my own photos for your office at Paradise Lodge."

Gray had to fight the urge to smirk. "You're very bossy today."

"Yes, well, I'm starting to feel more like myself. Let's track down Regina and see if I can be bossy with her. I would like something to report back to Angela in case she shows up tonight."

"Do you think she will?"

Hali shrugged. "I have no idea. I would prefer to be prepared, though."

"I think that's a solid plan."

ESPRESSO YOURSELF WAS ONE OF THOSE cutesy coffee shops with eight different types of milk offerings and thirty different flavor options. It was located directly on the beach, with a nice view, and was sandwiched between two resorts and public beach access. That meant it was a busy place.

Because of the foot traffic coming in and out, Hali and Gray were at a loss as to how they should approach Regina.

"You're sure that's her?" Hali asked as they sipped iced tea in the shade and watched the woman in question.

"Yup." Gray held up his phone so Hali could see the screenshot he'd taken of Regina's driver's license. It was definitely the same woman, although she'd put on a few pounds and let her hair grow longer.

"How do you want to do this?" Hali asked.

"I honestly don't know." Gray glanced around the coffee shop. There were ten people spread out at various tables in a small space. There were also two other workers. There was nowhere to have a private conversation, even if Regina would agree to sit down and talk to them. "Maybe we should wait until the end of her shift and follow her into the lot."

"That's kind of creepy."

"Do you have a better idea?"

Hali blew out a sigh as she considered her options. Rather than respond to Gray, she waited until Regina walked by after delivering a drink. She was quick and precise when she snagged the sleeve of the woman's shirt.

"We need to talk about Angela Brennan," Hali announced.

Gray slapped his hand to his forehead. "You are almost never smooth when it comes to this stuff," he complained. "I don't know why I expect you to be smooth, but you never are."

"It's a mystery," Hali agreed. She was calm when meeting Regina's panicky gaze. "We don't want to cause trouble. We just want to talk."

"How did you find me?" Regina blurted.

"It wasn't that difficult," Gray replied. "If you talk to us, I'll give you some tips on how to hide yourself better."

Regina hesitated, touching her tongue to her top lip, then she nodded. "It cannot be in here. I get off in fifteen minutes." She inclined her head toward the beach. "See that little shaded area there, the spot with the tables and umbrellas?"

Gray nodded.

"I will meet you out there when I finish here."

"Okay." Gray's smile was easy. "We'll take refills before we go."

"Fine." Regina glared at him. "You'd better have some really good tips."

"I'm a professional," Gray replied. "You'll be shocked at what I can help you do."

HALI HATED BAKING IN THE HEAT, AND EVEN though they were in the shade, she was sweating profusely when the fifteen minutes was up.

"Okay, she can come out here at any time," she complained.

Gray chuckled. "She can't make it obvious. Give her a second."

"She's probably not even coming out here," Hali said. "She probably made us walk out here because she knows we won't be able to get back to the parking lot in time to stop her when she drives off."

Gray opened his mouth to tell her she was being ridiculous. Then he thought better of it and straightened. His gaze moved to the parking lot for a beat, and then he turned back to Hali. "Up," he ordered as he stood.

Hali stood without hesitation. She wasn't surprised when he slid his arm around her waist and hoisted her up. "You think we've been had, don't you?"

"Let's just say I'm not taking any chances." Gray jogged through the sand, grinning as Hali made grunting noises as he jostled her. "Those noises would be a turn-on under different circumstances," he noted.

"You're kind of a pig," Hali complained.

"I'm okay with that." Gray was out of breath when he reached the parking lot and had to lower Hali so he could calm himself. He wasn't looking up, but down, when Hali made an excited noise. "What?" he asked as he raised his chin.

Hali pointed, drawing his attention to the opposite end of the lot. There, Regina was scurrying toward an older model Ford Focus.

Gray stepped forward without thinking. "Regina, wait!" he called out.

Regina glanced up, met his gaze, and then did the one thing Gray wasn't expecting and threw a bolt of magic at him. It happened so fast, Gray was caught unaware and spun in the air. He hit the pavement. Hard.

"Gray!" Hali moved as quickly as she could to get to him. Her eyes were filled with concern when they locked with his. "Are you okay?"

"I'll survive," he replied. Everything hurt from the blow.

"Okay, I'll be right back." Hali turned and headed toward the car Regina was climbing into.

Gray was still dazed and confused, but he managed to register that Hali was making the wrong move even from his position on the ground. He pushed himself forward and managed to gain his feet just in time to grab Hali before Regina could run her over. For good measure, Regina threw more magic at them as she made her escape. Hali was aware enough to deflect it into the sand.

"What the hell?" Hali complained when Gray put her on the ground. "I had her exactly where I wanted her."

Gray almost laughed. He caught himself though. "If you mean you wanted her to run you over, then yes, you had everything under control."

Hali threw her hands in the air. "She's gone, Gray."

"That means she wasn't going to talk to us regardless. Did you realize she was a witch? I mean ... we talked to her inside. You didn't mention her being a witch."

The question caught Hali off guard. "I didn't sense anything. It's possible she was shielded, though."

"Cammie didn't mention her being a witch either," Gray noted.

"Maybe she didn't know." Even as Hali said it, the assumption didn't feel right. "It's weird there are three witches, all of whom knew each other, and all without a coven."

"How do you know they were without a coven?"

"I guess I don't. That's what makes the most sense, though."

Gray ran his hands over her head to smooth her hair, which was now as wide as it was long thanks to the humidity and excitement. "Let me ask you something, Hali, could all three of these witches be working together?"

Hali found the question difficult to answer. "Maybe they used to work together," she said finally. "Maybe they were all involved in something back then, and when Angela got arrested, it hit a little too close to home. Maybe that's why Cammie and Regina went into hiding."

"That makes sense. Do you think Cammie was snowing us about finding her calling?"

"She seemed sincere enough. Her mother said Cammie wasn't at the trial, though, and Cammie said she was. I found that suspicious. Anything is possible I guess."

Gray motioned for Hali to move to his truck. He opened the passenger door for her and lifted her without prompting. Her hip wasn't in good enough shape for her to pull herself up. "Hali, do you think it's possible that Cammie and Regina set Angela up for something they did? Like ...

maybe Cammie feels guilty about it and that's why she's working at the clinic."

"I can't rule that out, but Cammie seemed pretty sincere," Hali said.

"So did Angela."

"Yeah." Hali rubbed her cheeks. "I don't know, Gray," she said finally. "I need to think on it."

"Maybe we should talk to your grandmother. She knows a lot about covens ... and she knows about witches who aren't in covens."

"She might have some dirt," Hali agreed. "It can't hurt to talk to her. We're going to have to head back to Tampa, though."

"Yeah. It's been a long day. It looks as if it's about to get longer."

"Do we have a choice?"

"Not that I can think of."

"Then let's do it. The sooner we get answers, the sooner we can get to moving your office to the resort. I'm looking forward to that."

"You just want to gossip with Joan."

"That, too. I like the idea of you being close, though."

"You just want to pick the photos I put on my desk."

"I'm going to look really cute."

He gave her a smacking kiss. "You always do."

14
FOURTEEN

Martha Moore was the sort of woman nobody messed with. It wasn't just because she was in charge of Tampa's most powerful coven either. It was just her. She did what she wanted, and nobody messed with her.

Well, mostly.

It seemed Rusty was still hanging around and messing with her. He was doing it shirtless, too.

Hali sat in the passenger seat of Gray's truck, arms folded over her chest, and glared at the man she considered a brother through the window. "What is he doing here?" she gritted out.

Gray was at a loss as he stared in the same direction and tried to wrap his head around the scene playing out in Martha's front yard. "He appears to be digging," he said finally.

Hali made a ridiculous face. "Really?" Her tone was icy. "I guess that's what the shovel is for. Why isn't he wearing a shirt?"

"It's hot out," Gray replied simply. "You work up a sweat when you're digging, and if it's already hot out, you need to air out things that sweat."

"What sort of things sweat, Gray?" Hali's tone was deceptively mild, but Gray recognized the challenge in her eyes.

"Baby, I'm not answering that. I'm not an idiot."

"Your brother is an idiot."

Gray cast a worried look toward Rusty. "It's possible he's just a nice guy offering his help to a sweet older lady."

"She could be his grandmother."

"So? Are you saying he can't help someone who is old enough to be his grandmother?" Gray opted to start playing offense. "I mean ... is he just supposed to ignore her if she asks for help?"

"He's supposed to keep his shirt on and not do ... whatever it is they're doing."

Gray had to hold back a sigh. "You don't know that they're doing anything."

"Did he tell you they're doing something?" Hali was suddenly suspicious.

"No, he did not," Gray replied. "To be fair, though, he would not tell me if they were actually doing something."

"Why?"

"Because he would prefer torturing me with not knowing."

"Which is exactly what he's doing now," Hali seethed.

"What do you want me to do about it?" Gray decided he would kill her with reasonableness if he had to. "What is it that you want me to do to fix this for you?"

"I want you to make sure your brother isn't having my grandmother ... stroke his ego."

Gray had to press his lips together to keep from laughing. "I see," he said finally, when he was reasonably assured he could speak without bursting out laughing. "Does your grandmother like stroking egos?"

"I'm not answering that."

"Fine." Gray pushed open the door. "We're here for a reason, Hali. I don't think obsessing about my brother's sex life is going to get us anywhere."

"Oh, so you *do* think they're doing it." Hali was appalled. "I'm never going to be able to look Rusty in the eye again. You know that, right?"

"This is a worry for another time," Gray insisted. "We need to focus on the problem at hand."

"Fine, but I know something weird is going on here."

Gray didn't say it out loud, but he was starting to wonder the same thing. It was one thing for Rusty to play games and mess with people's heads. How would Rusty have known that he and Hali were coming for a visit today, though? If he wasn't there to irritate people, then why was he there?

"This is a surprise." Martha beamed at her granddaughter as Hali determinedly eyed the slope of her grandmother's driveway. Martha lived in an older Tampa neighborhood, and the pavement wasn't level or smooth like in the newer parts.

Gray started toward Hali and then stopped himself. It was his natural instinct to slip in and help her. She wouldn't want that, though. Not in front of her grandmother. Instead, he kept a close eye on her, but didn't invade her space.

"You look like you're getting around better," Rusty noted as he leaned on his shovel and watched Hali's progress. "Slow and steady, huh?"

Hali glared at him. "It's going to take time for me to fully heal. I'm doing my best."

"I was not giving you a hard time." Rusty's eyes flashed with a mixture of amusement and annoyance. "What are you guys doing here? Other than checking up on us that is? Wait ... did you find Russell?"

"Believe it or not, we're not here for you," Gray replied.

"I don't believe it," Rusty replied. "I'm the center of your world and we both know it."

"If you say so." Gray turned his smile toward Martha. "We are here to see you, though."

"Is it serious?" Martha turned her gaze to Hali, who was eyeing the final incline up her grandmother's sidewalk with the sort of resigned sadness that made them all hurt. "Hali, dear—"

Before Martha could finish, Gray swooped in and lifted Hali the final few feet. Martha's yard was completely uneven, to the point where it was essentially dangerous to go walking across it for someone like Hali.

"I'm working on it," Rusty said to Gray's unasked question. "We're trying to even things out so the next time a hurricane blows through, there won't be so many pockets of water." Rusty rolled his neck. "It's more work than I thought, though."

"Maybe you would find your strength if you put on your shirt," Hali suggested.

Rusty shot her an amused smile. "Maybe you should take your shirt off so you can see what I'm dealing with."

Gray jabbed a finger in his brother's direction. "Do not take this to a weird place," he ordered.

Rusty's grin only widened. "You're so easy. As for you..." He watched as Hali leaned against the outside wall of her grandmother's house to catch her breath. "You're making progress, huh?" he said finally, changing course without a moment of hesitation. He was fond of Hali. More importantly, his brother loved her. He loved his brother. The key to Gray's happiness was Hali. No matter how much Rusty liked messing with people, he would never want anything but the best for his brother.

"It's been an interesting few days," Hali admitted.

"Let's take this conversation into the shade," Martha suggested. "I have a feeling you guys aren't here because you're bored."

"Not even a little," Hali agreed.

It took about ten minutes for Rusty to get cleaned up, Martha to gather the iced tea, and for everybody to get settled on the back patio. Martha had installed huge fans to keep the air circulating in that area, and Hali was more than happy to point her face toward one and pretend it wasn't sweltering out.

"So, what's up?" Rusty asked as he sat. "Does this have something to do with what happened with the prisoners?"

Gray nodded. "It's a long story. You'd better settle in." He was the one who filled in Martha and Rusty on everything that had happened. Hali sat in silence and drank her iced tea, her gaze constantly flicking back and forth between her grandmother and Rusty. When he was finished, he leaned back and waited for their reactions.

"Wait...so this witch is threatening to take you over again if Hali doesn't prove she's innocent?" Rusty demanded. "How does she expect Hali to do that?"

"I don't think she cares about the how," Hali replied. "She just wants it done." She leaned down and rested her face on the cool metal of the table. Suddenly, she was exhausted.

"Well, that's just crap," Rusty exclaimed. "You can't just come up with an acquittal out of thin air."

Martha, who had been quiet for the duration of the conversation, fixed Gray with a steely-eyed look. "Do you think she's innocent?"

"I have no idea," Gray replied. "I haven't even seen the original case files. I contacted Andrew to get them, but since it wasn't his case, he's having issues. The other detective is suspicious."

"And rightfully so," Rusty said. "Nobody should be trying to clear the prisoners. They should just be catching them. How many more are still out there?"

"Five," Gray replied. "Andrew texted me an update a few hours ago. He knows what's going on with Angela. He went with Hali to interview the mother and the cellmate. They have no leads on Angela right now, though. They do have a few leads on the others, and he expects another two to be in custody shortly."

"And Angela actually caught that woman who killed her children for you?" Rusty demanded. "What's up with that? It makes no sense."

"I don't know what to tell you." Gray held out his hands. "It's possible she is innocent and isn't as bad as everybody suspects. Or it's possible she's doing this to force Hali's hand. I don't know what the correct answer is."

"What about you?" Rusty turned his attention to Hali. "What do you think?"

"I don't know." Hali's forehead creased with concentration. "I don't get a good vibe from her."

Gray got up from the table without prompting and disappeared inside. Nobody said anything while he was gone—Martha and Rusty were still absorbing all the new information—and when he returned, he had a bag of ice with him.

"I'm fine," Hali said automatically.

"You're not fine." Gray was stern. "You're in pain. That's why you couldn't make it up that last incline. You've been on your feet way too much today."

"I don't need to be treated like a baby." Hali said it in a petulant voice but didn't push away the ice when Gray pressed it to her hip.

"You're acting like a baby," Martha countered.

Hali made a huffy noise.

"I get that you want to be back to a hundred percent, but that takes time," Martha chided. "A grown-up would be accepting the ice and admitting when she needs to rest so as not to push back her recovery."

"I don't have time for that," Hali countered. "I can hear a clock ticking in the back of my head. Angela will come for Gray. I know she will."

"Then maybe she's not the good person she wants you to believe," Martha said. "After all, just because she says she's innocent, that doesn't mean she's telling the truth. A good person does not blackmail another good person into doing her bidding."

Martha reached over and tapped Hali's wrist to get her attention. "Hey. She recognized that Gray was your weak spot, and she keeps going after him. That doesn't suggest she's a good person."

"I don't think she is a good person," Hali admitted. "The thing is, I don't know that I believe she's guilty of what she was accused of doing. Maybe she's a bad person who has done other bad things and she somehow thinks it's okay because she wasn't caught doing those other bad things."

"What are you going to do?" Rusty asked. "How can we help?"

"Well, there are three witches out there—all from Tampa—without a coven," Gray replied. "We were hoping Martha might have some information on that. Cammie and Regina are running around out there with magic—and Regina, literally, couldn't get away from us fast enough. Maybe there's something bigger involved."

"I don't know about that part, but those three used to be part of a coven," Martha offered.

Hali lifted her head, her interest piqued. "How do you know that?"

"Because I know the grandmother. Not Regina's grandmother. I actually have never heard of her. However, I do know the grandmother of the twins."

Well, now she had Hali's full attention. "Who is she?"

"Her name is Nancy Carter. She was younger than me by about seven or eight years. She was a member of our coven when I was growing up and coming into my magic. She was extremely gifted, but she had a moral line that was set somewhat farther south than mine."

"Meaning she liked dark magic," Hali surmised.

Martha nodded. "She did. She enjoyed making people squirm. She got off on making others subservient to her. She also wanted a place on the coven council."

"I'm surprised she didn't want your place in the coven," Gray mused.

"Oh, she did." Martha bobbed her head. "She was gunning for my position, but birth gave me a clear path to leadership. Nancy was an outsider who showed strong gifts, but she didn't have the birthright ... and that made her bitter."

"Did she try to kill you?" Hali asked. "I've never heard of this woman. Not a single story."

"She didn't try to kill me," Martha countered. "That's not to say that she wouldn't have gotten there eventually, but that wasn't her initial goal. She wanted a place on the board. I think her plan was to solidify her place there, make friends, and then come after me. She would've waited for me to make a mistake and then tried to slide in when I was vulnerable."

"Obviously, that didn't happen," Gray prodded.

"No. She got involved with a local warlock. Fred Tibbs."

Hali balked. "No way."

Gray darted his gaze to Hali. "Who is Fred Tibbs?"

"An evil warlock who got caught trying to rob a bunch of banks about forty years or so ago?" Hali looked to Martha for confirmation and continued when her grandmother nodded. "He used his magic—and a couple of other witches with somewhat saggy morals—to steal from a bunch of banks. He was eventually caught but died in the county jail when he was awaiting trial."

"How did he die?"

"The official story was that he hanged himself in prison," Martha replied. "Unofficially, however, the rumor is that the other witches who had been working with him managed to use mind magic to force a police officer to kill Fred for them."

Gray's mouth fell open. "You mean magic like what was used on me?"

"Unfortunately, I do." Martha held out her hands. "It sounds to me as if you were trying to fight the magic. That's why you moved slower than Angela was anticipating. That could be your strong character. It could be the shifter in you—

you have multiple types of shifter in your blood—but I can't be certain. Nancy's line was extremely strong with the mind magic, though. They used it to their advantage, and often."

"What happened with her?" Hali asked.

"She was about to be voted out of the coven when she quit to save face," Martha replied. "She saw the writing on the wall and took several witches with her. She went over to Clearwater and set up shop there."

"So, not close, but not too far away either," Gray said.

"My understanding is that Nancy sold dark magic spells to make money," Martha explained. "She didn't care about rules and regulations. She had a daughter, but the daughter was a dud. No magic."

"I've met the daughter," Hali confirmed. "There's definitely no magic there. She was also a crappy mother to her daughters."

"If Nancy had all this power—and two magical granddaughters—why didn't she take the girls in?" Gray asked.

"I can't answer that," Martha replied. "Nancy was never one to go out of her way for others. It's possible she decided to wait until the girls were adults so she wouldn't be forced to take care of them. Allowing those girls to grow up without anybody teaching them the ways of magic would've made them hard to control, though.

"I do know that Nancy's granddaughters joined her coven when they were in their late teens," she continued. "That news did filter to me right after it happened. We kept watch on Nancy from afar you see. We knew she was still a danger, even if she'd decided to leave this coven behind."

"Maybe that's why Angela went after Hali," Gray said. "She might've known the history between Nancy and you. Heck, maybe this is part of Nancy's revenge scheme."

"I don't think that's it." Martha was grave as she shook

her head. "Last I heard, Nancy was moved into an assisted living center. My understanding is that she doesn't have long to live. Whatever her granddaughter—or perhaps both granddaughters—is doing, she's not involved. Her power is waning."

"Do you know what home she's in?" Hali asked.

"I do." Martha bobbed her head. "I think perhaps you and I should talk to her." She sent an apologetic look toward Gray. "It would be better if you weren't there. I think this should be a meeting of the witches."

Gray looked torn. "I'm not thrilled at the idea of being away from Hali right now."

"We won't be doing anything strenuous," Martha assured him. "Nancy doesn't have the power to fight us off. Also, I think you and Hali could use a break from one another. You can't be on top of one another constantly. It's not healthy."

Gray opened his mouth to argue, but Rusty cut him off with a shake of his head.

"We still have a few places left on the list Mom and Dad supplied us with," he said. "A few of them are here in Tampa." He glanced at Martha. "You're not going to Clearwater, are you?"

"No," Martha replied. "Nancy is in town. I've had people watching the home in case it's a big ploy. It's not, for the record. She probably only has weeks—maybe even days—left."

"If you've been watching the home, have you been watching for other witches?" Hali asked.

"Yes, and one of my people sensed a witch outside yesterday," Martha replied. "Whoever the witch was sensed other witches watching and left. They didn't actually see her."

"I bet it was Angela," Hali mused. "Could she have made it in without you realizing? Maybe left and then shuttered herself when returning?"

"I would say no, but it sounds like Angela is strong, or at least stronger than she used to be," Martha replied. "I'm not sure. That's another reason we need to talk to Nancy. If she's set something in motion, we need her to tell us what it is."

"Will she, though?" Gray challenged. "I mean ... will she do what you want her to do? It sounds like she doesn't have a lot of love for you."

"She doesn't," Martha confirmed. "That doesn't mean there's no respect. It's been decades. I think we can have a conversation. She's too weak to do anything to us, though, Gray. There's no reason to get worked up."

Slowly, Gray slid his gaze to Hali. "Are you okay with this?"

"It seems like something that needs to be done," Hali said. "It can't possibly hurt."

"Are you okay with Rusty and me heading out to check a few locations while you're otherwise engaged?"

Hali nodded. She wasn't his mother. "Just be on the lookout for evil witches, huh?"

"I doubt they'll be going into the swamps with us," Rusty said. "It's fine. I'll watch him."

"Oh, the guy who has been doing weird stuff while shirtless with my grandmother, you're going to be watching him?"

Rusty merely winked at her. "That's what I said."

"Fine." Hali couldn't say no. It wasn't an option. "You guys do your thing. We'll do ours. I'll contact you when it's time to regroup," she said to Gray.

"That sounds good to me. Just be careful." Gray ran his

hand over her back. "Just because this witch is old and frail, that doesn't mean she doesn't have a trick left up her sleeve."

"You let me worry about Nancy," Martha said. "You worry about Russell. Maybe we'll be able to solve two problems today."

"Wouldn't that be a kick in the pants?"

15
FIFTEEN

Martha had to drive—Hali still wasn't cleared to drive anything bigger than a beachcomber, and she wasn't even comfortable doing that—which meant that there was no such thing as a steady speed. Martha either went ten miles over the speed limit, or twenty miles under it. There was no rhyme or reason as to which she chose on any given road.

Hali squeezed her eyes shut for much of the ride, and when they finally parked in the lot of Graceful Living Environment, she felt sick to her stomach.

"When was the last time they tested you for your license?" Hali demanded.

Martha blinked at her granddaughter. "Are you suggesting there's something wrong with my driving?"

"Oh, so many things," Hali muttered.

"You've always been a complainer. You're still my favorite granddaughter—not that you have a lot of competition—but you're a complainer. When are you going to outgrow that?"

Hali made a face. Her mother was an only child. "Why did you use the clarifier?" she demanded.

"I don't even know what you're talking about."

"You said granddaughter. *Daughter*. You only have three grandchildren total. For the record, I would never tell Annie that you like me more than her because that's just hurtful. But if I was your favorite overall, you would've said grandchild."

"I'm sure you're getting to a point somewhere," Martha drawled.

"I am," Hali confirmed. "Jesse is your favorite grandchild."

Martha's eyebrows, which were thin wisps that she filled in with a heavy hand most days, moved up her forehead. "That doesn't sound like a question."

"It's not a question," Hali confirmed. "It's a realization."

"Your brother is lazy," Martha countered. "He has potential should he ever get his head out of his behind. He's got a charming streak a mile wide."

"And you don't think I'm charming?"

"I think you're high strung," Martha countered. "You're not as high strung as your sister—nobody is—but you tend to clench your butt so tight some days I'm surprised you don't either lay eggs or poop diamonds."

Hali's mouth fell open. "I am not high strung."

"Of course you are. You always were. It's gotten worse since your accident."

"Take it back," Hali insisted.

"No. It's not my fault you clench so tight. Do you still grind your teeth? You were a teeth grinder when you were in high school."

"I'm not high strung." Hali practically screamed the

words as her grandmother turned off the engine of her oversized SUV. "Say it."

"Hali, only someone who is high strung would insist someone tell them that they're not high strung."

Hali had a feeling her grandmother was telling the truth. She didn't like it. "I don't think I can talk to you after this. We might need to take a break from one another."

"I can live with that." Martha picked a brisk pace when walking toward the front of the building. Hali tried to keep up, but she really was starting to drag. When Martha reached the door and looked over her shoulder to find Hali was just making it to the walkway, she got impatient. "Why can't you admit that you're hurting like a normal person?" she demanded as she returned to her granddaughter's side.

"Because admitting it hurts at my age is difficult," Hali replied. "I just want some semblance of control over my life. I haven't had that in forever it feels like. I just... I want to be okay."

Sympathy rolled over Martha's face. "You're going to be fine, Hali. You have to take it slowly, though. You're not a superhero."

"What happens if Angela comes for Gray, and I can't do anything but sit here?"

"Then you'll use your magic."

"What if she takes him and runs and I can't chase her?"

"Then you'll trip her."

"What if—"

"Hali, I'm not going to listen to a list of increasingly weird 'what if' scenarios. You'll handle what needs to be handled. That's what you do."

Hali wasn't convinced. "I'm afraid."

"I know you are." Martha took pity on her and linked her arm through her granddaughter's to help her up the remaining steps. "You don't like it when you're not the one in control. You need to be the big witch on the beach. Angela's skill set has you worried. You shouldn't let yourself get worked up, though."

"What if I can't help myself?"

"Then that's on you. Deep down, you know you're more than capable of handling this situation. It's not yourself that you're worried about. It's Gray. He'll never forgive himself if another person uses him to commit a crime. He does that butt-clenching thing, too. If you two ever clenched at the same time, I'm afraid you would form a black hole."

Hali murdered her grandmother with a single glare. "Do you think you're funny?"

"Most of the time," Martha confirmed.

"Well, you're not."

"You love me, and you know it." Martha held open the door for her granddaughter. "You haven't asked about Rusty," she said when Hali was halfway past her. "I know you have questions."

"Actually, I don't want to know what's going on with you and Rusty," Hali countered.

"Afraid the answer will traumatize you?" Martha was tickled pink at her granddaughter's response.

"Actually, I *am* worried that your answer will traumatize me," Hali confirmed. "If you two are doing the dance of darkness, I don't ever want to know about it."

Martha practically choked she was laughing so hard. "The dance of darkness? Seriously, how dramatic are you?"

"Dramatic enough that I would prefer living in an oblivious haze."

"Fine." Martha pointed her attention toward the woman at the front desk. "You let me do the talking."

"Why do you get to do the talking?" Hali challenged. "People like me. You intimidate them."

"Yes, but I'm old, and it makes sense that Nancy would be my friend. You have nothing tying her to you."

"Oh." Hali was sheepish. "I didn't think that far ahead."

"And that's why I'm the brains of the operation." Martha was in full control when she walked up to the woman behind the desk. "I'm here to see Nancy Carter."

The woman, a strawberry blonde with green eyes, flashed the sort of smile that normally made Hali uncomfortable. "Certainly. Are you a family member?"

"An old friend," Martha replied.

"Ms. Carter is currently only seeing family members."

"She'll want to see me," Martha countered.

"There's a notation in her chart that she only wants to see family."

"We were like sisters back in the day," Martha insisted.

"Still, rules are rules."

Martha narrowed her eyes to dangerous slits, and Hali had to hold her breath. She recognized her grandmother's expression. "Nancy is dying. I'm ancient and won't be far behind her."

"Don't say that," Hali protested. "I don't like it when you say things like that."

Martha ignored her. "I'll go to the newspaper and tell them that you're trying to keep two old ladies who are circling the drain from seeing each other when they're close to death. That you're stripping them of their dying wishes. Is that what you want?"

Hali had to bite the inside of her cheek to keep from laughing at the receptionist's horrified expression.

"Of course not," the woman said after several seconds. "It's just... Ms. Carter really isn't doing well."

"That's why I'm here," Martha replied. "We need to say our goodbyes. Are you really going to stop us from doing that?"

The receptionist looked caught. Then she focused on Hali. "Um ... and what are you doing here?"

"Making sure my grandmother doesn't die between here and the car," Hali replied without hesitation. "I'm just a chaperone of sorts. I don't really have anything to do with anything."

The receptionist let out a long-suffering sigh. "She's in room 214," she said finally. "Don't get me in trouble for breaking the rules."

Martha's smile was sunny. "I would never. Thank you so much for your time."

Hali offered up an apologetic wave before following her grandmother. "That was fairly mean," she said in a low voice. "You manipulated her."

"I can be way meaner."

Hali believed her.

Martha's shoulders were squared as she walked into Nancy's room. Things were quiet, the only sound coming from a pedestal fan, and the woman in the bed had long white hair that was spread out across her pillow like a tarnished halo. Her cheeks were sunken, her eyes rimmed in red with puffy bags under them, and the haunted look in the witch's eyes told Hali she really wasn't long for this world.

No, Nancy Carter didn't have much time left at all.

"I would say my eyes must be deceiving me, but I haven't been able to see well for three decades," Nancy offered by way of greeting. "You aged as poorly as I expected."

Martha smirked. "I'll have you know I have a thirty-year-old boy toy who thinks otherwise."

Hali was horrified. "Oh, don't tell her that," she squealed.

"There's that clenching thing again." Martha clucked her tongue and moved closer to Nancy. "So ... you're almost dead."

"You won't be ungodly far behind," Nancy replied.

"I think I still have a few good years in me left." Martha took Nancy's hand and clasped it hard. "I'm sorry it's come to this for you."

Hali had no idea of what to make of the showing between witches. They were enemies, and yet now that one of them was so close to death, they acted like the best of friends.

"Don't be," Nancy replied. "I should've listened to you. This is my karma." She gestured toward the otherwise empty room. It was nondescript and without an ounce of personality. There wasn't even a homemade afghan on the bed. "I thought I knew better than you back then. I thought you were too weak to do the hard things. Now I realize I was the one doing things the easy way. I never actually hung around to do things the hard way."

Martha looked pained. "You were powerful. Had you stayed, you would've landed in a high spot in the coven."

"And yet that wasn't good enough for me." Nancy let out a sigh, briefly shut her eyes, then focused on Martha again. "I don't have a lot of time left. If you're here to gloat, you'd better get started."

"I'm not here to gloat," Martha assured her. "I'm here about your granddaughters."

No surprise registered on Nancy's features. "Those girls were always destined for trouble. It's my fault. Laura should've been killed when she was still a toddler purposely trying to stick her tongue in light sockets."

Hali made a face. "That's a horrible thing to say about your daughter."

"Have you met her?" Nancy challenged.

"As a matter of fact, I have. She's ... limited."

Nancy snorted. "I would like to say she wasn't always that way, that it was the drugs that fried her brain. That's not how it is, though. She was always going to be a waste of space. I didn't help her of course—I didn't care about being a mother—so she never had a chance. I soothe myself with the knowledge that she was never going to amount to anything anyway."

Hali thought she should say something but was at a loss as to what.

"What about your granddaughters?" Martha challenged. "Were they always destined for loserdom too?"

"Actually, I think if I'd intervened and taken those girls, that maybe they could've grown up to be the sort of witches we'd both appreciate. That didn't happen, though. They're lost."

"We think Angela was here yesterday trying to see you," Martha admitted.

"I felt her." Nancy bobbed her head and swallowed. It looked as if it took a lot of effort. She had almost no strength left. "I don't know what she wanted. Last I heard, she was in prison."

"She escaped," Martha replied. "My granddaughter—this is Hali by the way—had the bad luck of running into her on the beach during the escape."

"Joyce's girl." Nancy looked Hali up and down. "I bet you're not a disappointment."

"She's kind of a whiner," Martha countered. "Other

than that, she's a good girl. She's strong, too. Angela is threatening her."

"For what?" Nancy looked genuinely perplexed. "Why would Angela escape from prison and go after your granddaughter?"

"I don't think she technically targeted my granddaughter," Martha replied. "Hali and her boyfriend just happened to be on the beach after dinner the night of the escape. That was a coincidence. Hali started helping the cops recapture some of the prisoners—from afar—and Angela saw it."

"Ah." Nancy nodded knowingly. "She wants Hali's magic."

"Well, maybe." Martha crossed her legs and readjusted in her chair. "During the melee—and I guess it was quite the mess—Angela used her magic to control Hali's boyfriend. He's not a normal human. He's a shifter."

"Oh, you let her hook up with a shifter?" Nancy looked appalled. "Why? They're mindless mooks."

Hali leaned forward. "Hey!"

Martha waved her hand to quiet her granddaughter. "She's just trying to get a rise out of you. Don't let her."

"I have to get my thrills somewhere," Nancy countered. "There are so few of them left. Literally."

"How long?" Martha asked.

"Days. Maybe hours at this point." Nancy shook her head. "Don't feel sorry for me. This is what I deserve. I had plenty of chances to change, and I didn't. You tried to make me see the light, and I refused. What's done is done.

"As for Angela, what does she want from you?" she asked Hali. "It must be bad for you two to be here asking me questions right before the end."

"I planned to come and visit you anyway," Martha countered. "I've had people watching the hospital. I was going to come tomorrow. Hali's visit moved up my timetable."

"You might've been too late tomorrow," Nancy noted.

"I'm here now."

"Yes. You are." Nancy squeezed her hand again. "Tell me about your interactions with Angela. She's always been the more unpredictable of the two. She's also the less intelligent. Cammie is the thinker."

Hali filed that information away to muse on later and gave Nancy a rundown of her interactions with Angela. She kept everything short and concise. Nobody had time for her to drag things out now.

"So, she wants you to prove her innocence, huh?" Nancy pursed her lips. "See, I would've bet money she was guilty."

"Maybe she is guilty," Hali argued. "Maybe she wants me to prove a negative."

"That sounds like something she would want," Nancy said. "You said Regina threw magic at you before escaping?"

Hali nodded.

"I honestly thought she was dead," Nancy admitted. "If Cammie was the thinker, and Angela was the woman with the plan, then Regina was the one who always ruined everything because she acted without thinking. She had the guts but never the glory."

"Meaning what?" Martha asked.

"Meaning that you can't trust any of them." Nancy stressed the words. "Whether they're working together or apart, none of them are trustworthy. They'll kill you just to steal your magic if they can."

"We don't have any reason to believe that they're working together," Hali admitted. "Angela's cellmate said she was always talking badly about Cammie, like she blamed her for Angela ending up in prison. When we talked to Cammie, she came right out and admitted she didn't want to see her sister."

"She probably doesn't," Nancy agreed. "Those two are like oil and vinegar. They don't mix. Unfortunately, they're tragically drawn together. Over and over again. One second they want to kill each other. The next they want to save each other. Their baser urges always win out, though. Together, they will never do the right thing. They'll just do the wrong things over and over again to claim victory over the other."

"Cammie said she found her calling, though," Hali insisted. "She likes helping people."

Nancy snorted. "You're obviously easily snowed if you believe that. My guess is, she's at that clinic because it gives her access to stuff like methadone. She's just as obnoxious as Angela. If she changed her name, it wasn't to hide from just Angela. It was to hide from someone else as well. It must be someone bad if she's been underground this long."

"Any idea who?" Martha asked.

"No. I've been out of their lives for years. We only briefly connected. I figured out they were magically strong and wanted to use them. They wanted to kill me and take control. I kicked them out. They took Regina with them."

"There's no proof Regina is working with them now," Hali said. "Is there a possibility they're all working against each other?"

"Definitely," Nancy answered without hesitation. "It's entirely possible that they're all going to try to hurt one another and take control of some kingdom only they believe exists."

"How do I combat the mind magic Angela has?" Hali asked. "I can't let her take over my boyfriend again. She'll make him do something horrible, and he'll never get over it."

"I can only think of one way in the short term," Nancy replied. She looked tired, as if the conversation was eating away at her stamina. "Open the top drawer of my nightstand." She inclined her head to the right.

Hali did as instructed and found what looked to be a sapphire runestone nestled next to a deck of playing cards.

"The nurses think that's fake, but it's real," Nancy said. "It's a powerful rune that I created when I was trying to control the girls."

Hali balked. "I don't want to control them. I just want to stop them."

"This might be your only way to do that." Nancy was calm. "I'm not giving it to you because I want you to control them. They have to be stopped, though. I taught them to be like me. The problem is, they were already like me. Now they're worse than I ever was."

"We don't want to kill them," Martha assured Nancy. "We just want to lock them away."

"You'd be better off killing them." Nancy was deadly serious. "They're never going to learn their lessons. Not even when they're old and gray like me. They'll hurt the world as much as they can. They'll hurt you. They'll never offer anything good to this world. You would be better off eradicating them."

"That's never going to be my first choice," Hali said. "I have to try to stop them first. Without killing them."

"The stone is your best chance. You'll be able to counteract any magic they throw at you."

"Is there anything I can do for you?" Martha asked. "You've helped us. I want to help you. Maybe I can try to get you sprung to my house for the end."

"Don't bother." Nancy's voice was weak. "It will be over soon. Just make sure the girls don't get my magic. If Angela was here, she wasn't looking to bond with her grandmother. She knows I'm close to dying and wants my powers. Don't let her get them."

"I'll stay with you," Martha promised. "Hali can call her sister or brother to get a ride. The least I can do is stick with you."

Nancy looked grateful. "I'm sorry I didn't listen."

"Neither of us listened," Martha replied. "Had we been willing to listen, we might've been able to find common ground. At least we found some before it was too late."

"Yes." Nancy closed her eyes. "Now, tell me about your boy toy. I think that's the last story I would like to hear before I shake off this mortal coil."

Martha's smile was very cat that ate the canary. "My pleasure."

16
SIXTEEN

The last Tampa location on the list—there were still a few outlying places to check, but Gray didn't want to risk heading that far out when Hali might need him—was in a neighborhood instead of being isolated. It wasn't the sort of place Gray would've chosen to hide, but they had to check it.

The neighborhood was rundown by Tampa's standards, and there were only three houses on a dead-end street. Despite his initial dubiousness, Gray found the hair on the back of his neck standing on end when they exited his truck down the street from the house in question.

"How come you're not asking what's going on with Martha and me?" Rusty asked. His nose was out of joint because Gray had talked about anything but Martha during the ride. This was their third stop, and his patience had worn out.

"Because I don't want to know."

"But ... I like her."

"Please." Gray made a face. "You might like her—heck,

you might even be attracted to her in a weird way—but you're not going to settle down with her."

"What makes you say that?" Rusty was offended. "She's awesome."

"Yes, and you want children one day. She might be powerful, but she's not *that* powerful."

"I do want children," Rusty confirmed. "I still like her."

"Or you just want some attention because you really like Carrie and that's going nowhere."

Carrie Radish was Hali's best friend. Rusty had met her months before and grown close with her almost immediately. Unfortunately for him, Carrie was a lesbian, and try as he might, he couldn't get her to cross into bisexual territory.

And he *had* tried. Numerous times.

"Carrie isn't an option for me," Rusty replied. "It pains me to say that—you have no idea—but I've tried. She doesn't even get a mild case of dry mouth when I take off my shirt."

"And Martha does?"

"Martha appreciates my beauty." Rusty fluttered his eyelashes in exaggerated fashion.

"Geez." Gray shook his head. "You are all kinds of weird. You know that, right?"

Rusty shrugged. "I find her stimulating to talk to. That's not easy for a guy like me."

"And why is that?"

"Because people look at me as a piece of beefcake and nothing more."

"If you want to be set up with someone, Hali might know some people. I would've suggested Mindy Grant—she's a server at the restaurant we like to have breakfast at—but apparently Andrew flips her switch."

"I might go after her just to steal her from Andrew, but I've met her. She seems fine. She's just not 'the one.'"

Gray slowed his pace and gave his brother his full attention, even though it took effort. "Are you looking for 'the one'?"

"Six months ago I would've said no. I'm jealous of you and Hali, though."

"You're jealous?" Gray was amused despite himself. "Since when?"

"You guys are happy. I mean...your favorite thing to do is cuddle up with her on the back patio and mess with the flamingo."

"I could do without the flamingo." Wayne, Hali's familiar, had been keeping a low profile of late. They'd only seen him a handful of times over the past few days. Gray was suspicious—he was always suspicious of the bird—but that was a problem for another time. "As for being happy, I am. I'm not sure you can set out to find 'the one' though. I think you need to let 'the one' find you."

"That's how it happened with you," Rusty mused. "You and Hali weren't looking for each other but couldn't stay away once you crossed paths."

"I fought the attraction I was feeling for Hali, and it grew painful. I'm not saying to ignore the possibility of stumbling across 'the one,' but if you put too much pressure on yourself, then you're going to settle, and I don't want to see that."

"You think I'm settling for Martha?"

Gray made a face. "You're not dating Martha. While I acknowledge that you might've done something dirty with her out of curiosity, you're just helping her because you find her funny and you're a good guy."

"I could be doing more with her," Rusty argued.

"You're just looking for attention."

"Be that as it may, don't you dare tell our parents that I'm not doing anything with Martha. I plan to take her to a family dinner at some point."

"You just want to see Mom's head spin around like that kid in *The Exorcist*."

"There are worse things."

Gray chuckled. Even though they were on a serious mission, he was amused. His brother always made him laugh. His laughter died quickly, though, when he saw a curtain move inside the house they were staring at. "Someone is in there."

"Yup." Rusty bobbed his head. "I've had a feeling someone has been watching us since we parked."

"What do we know about this house?"

"Just that it was often used as a safehouse for the pack. I don't see why anybody would be in there now. The pack is in disarray."

"So ... whoever is in there is hiding," Gray surmised. He rolled his neck and glanced around. The other two houses looked quiet. There were no vehicles in the driveway.

"What do you want to do?" Rusty asked after several seconds.

"I want to talk to Russell," Gray replied. "We cannot go inside that house, though. It's a trap."

"Definitely not," Rusty agreed.

Gray pressed his lips together, debating, and then he started walking again. He was calm as he stepped up to the front porch and knocked on the door.

Inside, everything was quiet. The curtains weren't moving, everything was silent, and yet there was tension oozing out of every crack.

"Let's end this," Gray said in a declarative voice. "I don't want to keep playing games, Russell. Are you a man or a mouse?"

"That's good," Rusty said. "Call his manhood into question. That won't go poorly."

Gray cast his brother a sidelong look. "Do you have a better idea?"

"Sure." Rusty picked up a planter from the front porch. The flowers inside were dead. He showed no hesitation before heaving it through the window. "We'll use fire next," he called through the broken glass. "If you have people in there protecting you, then they'll die too. Try not to be a little girl about this."

Gray worked his jaw. "You really shouldn't use phrases like 'little girl' as an insult. Women are just as powerful as men. That's demeaning."

Rusty pinned Gray with an incredulous look. "Are you being serious right now?"

"Yes. One day Hali and I are going to have kids. I hope one of them is a mouthy little witch who looks just like her mother. I will not allow anyone to use the term 'little girl' as an insult. That's wrong."

"Wow." Rusty shook his head. "Way to be sensitive, bro." He clapped Gray's arm. "Fine." He cocked his head, as if thinking. "Try not to be a Nickelback fan about this. I don't want to hear any crying."

The unmistakable sound of shuffling could be heard inside, then the house door opened.

Russell Greason had been in hiding for less than two weeks and yet he looked as if he'd aged ten years. He had a full beard, and his hair was shorter. Both were streaked with white, making Gray wonder if he'd been dying both to keep up appearances before his unceremonious fall.

"Russell," Gray said dryly. "You look rough."

"Not like a little girl, though," Rusty said.

Russell took a step back. "You might as well come in."

Gray immediately started shaking his head. "Yeah, I'm not doing that. You can come out." He stepped off the front porch and onto the yard. "You can't run. We'll call for backup and have half the pack down here in five minutes flat. You can't fight, because even though I'm guessing you have a few bodyguards with you, they're likely not going to be willing to die for you. It's best you come out here for the discussion that needs to be had."

Russell looked over his shoulder, clearly making eye contact with someone. He was resigned when he stepped out. "Are you going to kill me here?"

"That's not my intention," Gray replied. "You need to turn yourself in to the pack."

"So they can kill me?" Russell sneered. "Why would I possibly want to do that?"

"Because you don't have a choice," Gray replied. "Right now, your power over the pack has to be ceded. You can either do that willingly and live—"

"As an outcast." Russell's bitterness was palpable.

"It's either that or die," Gray replied evenly. "I've lived as an outcast my entire adult life. It's not so bad."

Two figures appeared on the porch. They were big, hulking shifters Gray recognized. "Roarke. Grim." Gray nodded in greeting. "Are you guys going to hitch your wagon to him for good?"

The two shifters exchanged looks but didn't reply. That allowed Gray to turn his attention back to Russell.

"I told you what would happen if you moved against Hali," he said in a low voice. "You claimed that wasn't your intention. Then your buddies tried to take over the beach."

"Yes, and you managed to rally a whole other pack to

fight your battle," Russell shot back. "I don't suppose you'd like to tell me how that came about, would you?"

"Frankly, it's none of your business," Gray replied. "The simple fact of the matter is that they wanted to protect the area from the merrow as much as I did. I didn't make a deal with them. I didn't put your pack at risk. I simply told them what was happening and how I wanted to combat it."

"In other words, he wasn't a sneaky sneak," Rusty said. "Unlike you, who sent members of our pack to die while you went into hiding."

"The merrow were powerful," Russell argued. "They would've killed me."

"And we won't?" Rusty was having none of it. "You wanted Hali dead because you thought that would hurt Gray. You were afraid that his station was being elevated too much thanks to the work he was doing with Hali, and this was all a ploy for you to maintain power you didn't deserve in the first place."

Grim made a growling sound behind Russell.

"Don't attack them," Russell instructed. "We need to finish this conversation. I think they can be reasoned with."

"Yeah, I don't think he was going to attack me," Rusty replied. "I'm guessing he doesn't know all the facts about the little maneuver you pulled, so what I just said caught him by surprise. I'm sure you told him a different story than the rest of us saw with our own eyes."

Roarke stirred. "We were under the impression that Gray was working with the merrow."

It took everything Gray had not to explode. "Do you really think I would work with the creatures that were threatening my girlfriend?"

"We heard she used magic to enslave you and that you wanted her dead," Grim argued.

Gray's eyes narrowed, and he had to grip his hands into fists at his sides lest he start throwing punches at Russell. That would result in a big fight, and he was determined to put an end to this as peacefully as possible. "That is not true. Hali is a good person."

"She's a witch," Russell snapped. "You shouldn't be with a witch. I know people have been making noise about you taking over the pack, but you can't put a witch in charge of our people."

"I don't want to take over the pack," Gray countered. "I have never wanted that."

"And yet you fought with the elders."

"I fought with people who were trying to marry off a teenage girl—against her will mind you—to a decrepit old man who wanted nothing more than to use her as a toy," Gray growled. "I am not going to apologize for that. Our pack is buried in the past, in the old ways. Our pack won't survive unless you look to the future and move forward."

"And how do we do that? By revering women?" Russell rolled his eyes. "We heard you admonishing Rusty about using the term 'little girl.' You're weak. I won't be part of a weak pack."

"That's probably a good stance because you're not going to be invited to remain in the pack," Rusty said. "You stole pack money."

Grim took an inadvertent step forward. "What?"

"You went into hiding because you knew that the pack would be left floating because they couldn't name a new leader," Rusty continued, refusing to veer from the subject at hand. "Your plan was to let the pack flounder and then swoop back in when people were at their worst to try to hold on to your leadership position. That's not going to happen."

"And what are you going to do?" Russell challenged. "There are three of us and two of you. You can't fight us."

"I can take both of them," Rusty countered. He flashed a winning smile toward Roarke and Grim. "No offense. I like you guys, and I hate that you've been used, but we're not letting him get away again."

Roarke and Grim looked at one another for a second time. Gray sensed a softening in their stance ... and not toward Russell.

"What will you do with him if we give him to you?" Roarke asked finally.

"What?" Russell's face drained of color. "You can't be serious."

"Shut up," Grim snapped. "We're talking to them."

Rusty's smugness came out to play. "We'll take him to the pack. In fact, we won't even take him into our custody. We'll call for the pack to pick him up and then we'll let justice play out that way."

"We don't want to kill him," Gray offered. "Actually, given what he tried to do to my girlfriend, I kind of do want to kill him. I won't, though, because it's not the best thing for the pack."

"Are you going back to the pack?" Roarke asked. "Will you take his place?"

The question threw Gray. "I have no intention of going back to the pack."

"Don't listen to him," Russell snapped. "He wants to take my position. This is all a way for him to snow you guys into believing he's some benevolent ruler. He's pretending he doesn't want the position. Then, when he gets it, he'll be ruthless."

"He's lying," Gray countered. "I don't want to be part of the pack. I was ostracized at a young age. I've made my way in the world without the pack. There's no going back for me because I've made my life separate from the pack.

"I love my witch, and I want to be with her," he continued. "I would never subject Hali to the rules of the pack—she can't live that way—and I'm not going back without her. I don't want Russell's job."

"And yet you sound as if you're the exact right person for it," Roarke countered.

"I'm going to work on him over the pack stuff," Rusty said. "I happen to think he would be a great leader, too. His head is extremely hard, though, and we need it to be his idea. That's not even important right now, though.

"What is important is that we get Russell back to the elders," he continued. "He took the pack money. It's going to take time to track it down. They need to dole out his punishment as the pack sees fit. This isn't just about Gray."

This time when Grim and Roarke looked at one another, they were determined.

"We'll help." Grim grabbed the back of Russell's shirt and practically lifted him off the ground. "Call the retrieval team. We'll wait."

Russell kicked out, trying to find purchase with his foot, but he couldn't. "Put me down! I'm still your master. You have to do what I say."

"No, you were our master," Roarke replied. He almost looked bored now. "We were considering killing you ourselves. We were tired of being on the run." He flicked his eyes to Rusty. "He's had us moving between houses ever since the thing went down on the beach. He claimed it was a conspiracy against him—and we believed him—but we were starting to have doubts."

"You should have doubts," Rusty said. He already had his phone out. "I'll make the call. It shouldn't take them long to get somebody over here." He was positively giddy as he locked gazes with Gray. "I guess this didn't turn out to be a waste of time after all. Mom and Dad came through."

"Your parents turned me in?" Russell was furious. "I'll kick them out of the pack first."

To Gray, Russell seemed like a petulant boy prince having a meltdown because he didn't get his way. He had no interest in feeding the childish monster, though. "My parents gave me a list of properties I might find of interest. They didn't know where you were. We've checked a good ten properties overall. We just happened to luck upon you today because we had a break in our schedule."

"I'm not going to go down without a fight," Russell warned him. "It's not going to happen. I'll reclaim my position in the pack. Just you wait."

"Good luck with that." Gray offered up a grimace to the other two shifters. "Don't let him run."

"We won't," Roarke promised. "We have families we want to see. We need this to be over."

"The retrieval team will be here in twenty," Rusty said as he disconnected. His demeanor was gleeful. "Then life is going to change for you, Russell. I can't wait to see what you look like behind bars."

"I'm going to call Hali," Gray said, taking a step away. "She needs to know I'm going to be at least two more hours."

"Knock yourself out." Rusty waved him off.

Gray took twenty steps away and pulled out his phone. Hali answered on the second ring. He thought he had the big news of the day. It turned out she did.

"Where are you now?" he demanded after hearing her story.

"Annie is driving me to the tiki bar. I'm going to check in there."

"Wait for me when you get there," Gray said. "It's going to be at least an hour and a half, probably longer. Don't go anywhere."

"Oh, I have no intention of going anywhere. I'm in pain and need some food. I'll wait for you. I promise."

"Good. I'll be there as soon as I can."

"Then you're buying me a big steak. I need the red meat to fuel me."

Gray chuckled despite the seriousness of their conversation. "Something tells me that can be arranged."

"That's exactly what I wanted to hear."

17
SEVENTEEN

Hali had a lot on her mind when she got to the tiki bar. Since she had a full staff of workers, she didn't need to worry about waiting on customers. That didn't stop her from sitting in a chair inside the hut and complaining to her best friend Carrie, who had the night off and was looking for a drink. Carrie sat on a stool outside, sipped her blue cocktail, and listened to Hali rant and rave about evil witches and shifters for twenty minutes through the window before she lifted a finger to silence her friend.

"What?" Hali asked, her forehead creasing.

"When was the last time you had sex?" Carrie asked.

The question, for obvious reasons, threw Hali. "Excuse me? What does that have to do with anything?"

"I'm just curious." Carrie took another sip. "Are you allowed to have sex with your hip?"

"That's none of your business." Hali didn't consider herself a prude, but she couldn't believe Carrie had the audacity to ask her that with so many other people around.

"Please." Carrie was having none of it. "The first time

you and Gray did the musty mambo, you and I spent three hours over cocktails dissecting it." She cocked her head. "I think you're wound so tight because you're not having sex."

"When was the last time you had sex?" Hali fired back.

"Last night."

"You've been seeing someone? I thought you were between girlfriends."

"You don't need to be committed to have sex."

"Whatever." Hali leaned back in her chair. "Gray is worried he's going to hurt me. There's been flirting ... and petting ... but nothing intense because he's convinced that he's going to set back my recovery."

"Does that irritate you?"

"I'm fine," Hali replied. "I am perfectly fine."

Carrie chuckled. "You need to take the edge off. Sleeping next to your big hunk of a man when he won't make a move has to be tiresome."

"If you haven't noticed, we have other things going on in our lives."

"Yes. Evil witches and shifters. It sounds to me as if one of your big problems just got removed."

Hali wasn't certain that was true. "The shifters want Gray to be their new pack leader." She didn't realize she was going to say it until the words were already out of her mouth. Once they escaped, however, she felt better about things. Lighter somehow.

"Really?" Carrie pressed her lips together and considered it. "I think he would make a good pack leader. He would be able to bring the pack into the modern age. You don't like this idea?"

"No."

"Why not?"

"Because Gray doesn't want to be the pack leader."

Carrie waited. She knew there was more to it than just that. She sipped her cocktail and eyed Hali with the sort of intensity that she knew would make her friend uncomfortable.

"Pack leaders are only supposed to be with other pack members," Hali said finally.

"And there it is." Carrie grinned. "Are you worried Gray will dump you if he becomes pack leader? Because—and this is said with as much love as possible—you're a crackhead if you believe that."

"That's said with love?" Hali's eyes flashed. "You need to work on your sweet talk."

"I didn't have any complaints last night. I also didn't say it to offend you. I've seen you two together, though. Gray is never going to love anybody but you."

"Maybe not." Hali felt Gray's love to her very marrow. "He is the type to do what he feels is necessary for the greater good, though."

"And why would marrying you be a detriment to the pack?"

"Because I'm not a shifter. I don't understand their ways."

"Why is that a bad thing?" Carrie sounded like a clinical psychologist now. "Maybe you could help Gray turn the pack into something better."

"But ... he says he doesn't want it."

"I think you just don't like change." Carrie finished off her drink and handed the empty cup to Hali. "I'll have another if you don't mind."

Hali rolled her eyes but grabbed the cup. She made a huffy noise as she stood, then grunted as she leaned forward to balance herself on the bar.

Carrie, who might've been in the mood to mess with

her friend, was instantly alert. "What is it? Do you need to go to the emergency room? I can't drive—I'm a little tipsy—but I can find someone else to drive."

"It's not that," Hali assured her. "I've just been on it more today than I have been since the surgery. Yesterday too. Sitting down probably wasn't the best idea. I'll be fine. The doctor told me to expect this as I increased my activity level."

Carrie didn't look convinced. "I'm calling Gray." She already had her phone out when Hali stared glaring daggers into her.

"Don't you dare call Gray. I'll hex you to smell like patchouli if you do."

Now it was Carrie's turn to make a face. "You know how I feel about patchouli."

"That's why I said it. Don't call Gray."

"Who isn't calling Gray?" a male voice asked, causing both Hali and Carrie to yelp in surprise. Hali's hand went straight to her hip when she pushed herself up to see the space beyond Carrie.

Gray, Rusty at his side, arched an eyebrow as he looked between them. When his gaze fell on Hali, and how she was favoring her hip, he went straight to the hut opening and headed for the ice machine.

"Great," Hali muttered when she saw him filling a baggie. "Just great."

"Sorry." Carrie's smile was sunny. She didn't look sorry. "Hey, stud." Her grin turned wicked when she pointed it at Rusty. "Where have you been?"

"Spending my time with a woman who understands the wonder that is Rusty," he replied as he hopped onto the stool next to her. "I'll have what she's having," he said to Hali.

"You're going to hold on." Gray wrapped his arm around Hali and pulled her back to the chair, where he proceeded to make clucking noises as he pressed the ice against her aching hip. "And you're going to sit here until I'm certain you're not in pain."

Hali wanted to be annoyed—she was an adult for crying out loud—but she couldn't be. "I just overdid it today," she said in a low voice when he pressed his forehead to hers. "I'm okay."

"I still want to take care of you," Gray replied. "That's my favorite thing to do."

"Gag me." Rusty rolled his eyes as he stood and let himself into the tiki hut. "You guys just get grosser and grosser. What are you going to do when there are little ones added to the mix?"

"I'm going to spoil them rotten," Gray replied. "What are you doing?" He shot his brother a dirty look.

"There's no way I'm drinking anything that you make—you lack imagination when it comes to cocktails—and I'm not waiting for Hali. Move your butt." Rusty playfully knocked his brother to the side. "I'm going to make drinks for both of us," he said to Carrie. "Then I'm going to tell you about my new boo. She appreciates me … unlike you."

"Oh, so she likes back hair," Carrie drawled. "I knew you would eventually find a woman who would warm to your particular form."

"I don't have back hair." Rusty glared at her. "Stop saying that."

Carrie was blasé. "If that's your story."

"I'll take my shirt off right now." Rusty reached for the back of his shirt, but Gray slapped his hand away.

"We're in a place of business," Gray snapped. "You

know that saying 'no shirt, no shoes, no service'? That applies here."

"It can't apply here," Rusty argued. "We're on the beach. During the day, half the dudes don't wear shirts."

"Leave your shirt on." Gray turned back to Hali. "How are you?"

"I'm concerned," Hali replied. She figured now was not the time to start lying. "Nancy told us some troubling stuff."

Gray glanced around. "Where is Martha? I'm surprised she left you if the news was all that bad."

"Nancy is dying. Soon. Grandma is sitting with her until the end."

"If what Nancy told you is so bad, why aren't you preparing?" Gray demanded.

"For what? I mean ... what are we supposed to do? If Angela is going to come, she's going to come." Hali thought about the rune stone she had safely tucked away in her pocket. "Nancy did give me something that should hopefully cut off the mind magic that Angela can call so easily. We still don't have a way to track them, though."

"What about a locator spell?" Rusty asked. He'd thrown six different types of liquor in the blender cup, and he didn't even look over when he asked the question. He was more intent on his masterpiece.

"We could try to cast a locator spell, but I think it's a waste of time," Hali replied. "Angela knows where we are. She wants something from us. I think that means she's going to come to us. The question is, will she be alone?"

Reality slapped Gray across the face. Hard. "You think she's working with Cammie and Regina."

"I think she could be working with one or both of them," Hali replied. "Cammie and Regina were in hiding for a reason. What if they were partners with Angela and they somehow turned on her for something they all did?"

"So, you don't think Angela is innocent?" Carrie asked.

"I have trouble seeing her as innocent given what she's willing to do with Gray to get her own way." Hali chose her words carefully. "A good person is still a good person deep down. I don't get the feeling Angela was ever a good person. Her grandmother confirmed that."

"It sounds to me as if Angela never had a chance to be a good person, though," Rusty argued. He poured the contents of the blender container into two cups and then tossed cherries and oranges on top of Carrie's before shoving it toward her. "Don't say I never gave you anything."

"You're just mad because I won't ask about your new boo," Carrie noted.

"You'll find out soon enough." Rusty's smile was sunny.

Irritated, Hali glared at his profile. "He's been hooking up with my grandmother," she blurted.

Rusty's mouth fell open. "What did I ever do to you? That was my secret to unveil when I was in the mood. Do I look like I'm in the mood?"

Hali shrugged. "I don't have time to play your childish games, Rusty. I think trouble is coming for us—in the form of three witches—tonight."

"Three?" Gray leaned against the bar, his back to Carrie, and focused his full attention on his girlfriend. "So, you do think they're all working together."

Hali shook her head. "I think they *were* working together when the drug dealer was killed. I'm willing to bet he wasn't Angela's boyfriend at all. I think they were all doing drug dealing things together.

"Cammie and Angela have solid mind magic, and I'm

guessing they're the ones who roped in the clientele," she continued. "Seth Rochester was the guy securing the drugs, or perhaps cooking the meth, however that works. I'm not up on all the drug stuff. I also don't know what Regina's forte was, but she obviously has magic at her disposal.

"My guess is that Seth ticked them off, and they all killed him, or one of them did it with the okay of the others. Then, when Angela was the one the cops targeted, my guess is that Cammie and Regina left her twisting in the wind. That would've been easier than making themselves look guilty."

Gray nodded in understanding. "That makes a weird sort of sense. Cammie and Regina went into hiding right after."

"They probably took whatever money they'd accrued, split it, and went their separate ways," Hali confirmed. "Now that Angela is out, she wants payback. I don't think they're going to be working together. The problem is, if they come here looking for Angela, they're not going to see me as a friend either."

"It's like a trashy drug-dealing soap opera," Carrie mused. "What are you going to do?"

"I'm going to let them come after me."

Gray didn't like her response one bit. "What now?"

"Oh, don't give me that look." Hali shook her head. "We can't chase them. It will take forever, and if we're too persistent, they'll leave the area."

"And that's a bad thing why?" Gray challenged.

"Because then they'll hurt other people."

"But ... Cammie seemed sincere." Gray couldn't let it go. "She said she found her calling."

"At a job that is likely paid off the books and gives her

access to the sort of stuff recovering drug addicts might like to get their hands on."

"Like methadone," Carrie surmised. "That makes sense."

"Cammie isn't any better than her sister I don't think. She might've tried at one time, but she might actually be worse. She got good at hiding who she was." Hali shifted the ice bag and briefly closed her eyes. The dull ache was easing, but they still had hours in front of them. "Nancy doesn't deny she was a bad grandmother. She could've taken them in when their mother proved to be unreliable, but she waited until they were adults to make contact. By then, it was too late. They had no respect for her."

"I'm not sure she deserved respect," Gray argued. "She could've saved them. She didn't. I don't feel sorry for her."

"She's not the type of woman who would expect you to feel sorry for her," Hali assured him. "She knows she made the wrong choices in life. She actually believes karma caught up with her." She removed the rune stone from her pocket. "She gave me this. It's a blood magic rune. It will help control the mind magic that Cammie and Angela will try to use when they get here ... and they *will* try to control you, Gray."

"Then that means they'll probably try to control me, too," Rusty said. "I plan on being here to make sure you guys are okay."

"Me, too," Carrie said. "You can't get rid of me now."

"I appreciate you guys hanging around." Hali meant it. "We don't know what Regina is capable of, so we'll have to keep a close eye on her. Cammie and Angela will assume they have control because of their mind magic. They won't know about the rune."

"I would still feel better if we had another presence here," Gray said. "Are you going to be mad if I call Vin?"

Hali shook her head. "No. I think that's probably a good idea. Even if he just hangs out in the shadows on the beach, we know the mind magic won't work on him. If something happens and the rune doesn't work, he'll be able to incapacitate you and Rusty without killing you."

"I happen to think I could take him," Rusty replied.

"You would." Carrie rolled her eyes. "What time do you think they'll come?" she asked Hali.

"After the bar closes. They'll watch us." Hali glanced out into the darkness. "They might already be watching us. They won't move on us until there are fewer people around, though."

"Okay, that means we have time to eat." Gray took control of the situation. "We'll get some food delivered down here. We'll act like four friends having a good time. Then we'll wait for them."

"And I'll be able to ask Rusty about seeing Martha naked," Carrie said. "It's a win for all of us."

"See. I knew you were jealous." Rusty's grin was serene. "You really should give me a chance. I think I can make you forget that you're a lesbian."

"Oh, it's just sad that you think that." Carrie shook her head. She didn't look all that upset. "Tell me about you and Martha, though. Do you plan to have a family?"

Rusty guffawed.

Since they were focused on each other, Gray could give Hali his undivided attention. "How about you and I take our dinner over to one of those daybeds and you can eat lying down, huh?"

"That's not very good for digestion," Hali countered.

"No, but it will be good for icing your hip."

Hali's shoulders slumped. "You're going to make a big deal out of this, aren't you?"

"Yup." Gray was solemn when he nodded. "Tonight is a big test for you. I want to make sure you get some rest before it happens."

"Carrie says I need to have sex," Hali blurted.

Genuine discomfort washed over Gray's features. "What? Why would she say that?"

"She says I'm wound too tight. I thought she was just being Carrie, but now I think she might be right."

"We do ... that." Gray's cheeks turned pink. "Why are we talking about this in front of people again?"

Hali was amused despite herself. "We haven't done that since the surgery. We've gotten close, but nobody has crossed the finish line."

"Hey, you always cross the finish line on my watch." Now Gray was appalled. "Don't tell anybody otherwise."

"I'm just saying, that when this is over, maybe we should celebrate how we used to."

"I can't if you're in pain." Gray opted for the truth. "That will crush me."

"I know, but I think we both kind of need it. We're doing nonstop foreplay, and it's time to reclaim our lives. I'm getting better. I'm going to keep getting better. Let's have some fun together tonight."

Gray stroked her hair away from her face. "Fine. If you want me to have sex with you, I will."

"Oh, listen to the smooth talker," Rusty drawled. "Now I see how you got her in the first place."

Gray ignored him. "I want to make sure you're not in too much pain when this is over with, though. I want to be smart about it."

Hali didn't argue with him. There was no point.

"They're not as strong as me, Gray. The mind magic could make things difficult, but I think I've got that handled. You need to have faith in me."

"I have faith in you more than anybody else."

"Good." Hali's smile was bright. "During dinner, when I'm on the daybed with the ice, you can talk to me about the pack thing. I want to make sure you're not making decisions because of what you think I want."

Gray was taken aback. "How did we get to that?"

"Carrie is multifaceted wise."

"I definitely think you should hex Carrie to smell like patchouli."

"It's on my list."

"That's my girl." Gray gave her a soft kiss. "As for the pack, there's nothing to talk about."

"You let me be the judge of that."

18
EIGHTEEN

Hali's workers cleared out the tiki bar. They wiped everything down, closed the weather windows on the hut, but left the door open in case Hali's group wanted to go inside and make more drinks. Hali could tell they had questions, but they left her to deal with what was coming on her own.

At this point, even those who didn't know the whole truth about Hali recognized that weird things often happened around her. They did not want to insert themselves into her business.

"It's a nice night," Rusty noted as he sipped his beer. He wasn't drunk—and he had no intention of getting drunk—but he wanted to appear at ease.

"It's not as hot as it has been," Gray agreed. "That's nice, huh?" He turned his attention to Hali, who still had an ice pack pressed to her hip.

She, however, was not in the mood to talk about the weather. "Carrie thinks it would be good for you to be pack leader because you're more of a moderate," she persisted. "I didn't want you to consider it because I was convinced that would mean you would dump me, but now I'm wondering if I'm being fair to you."

Gray's expression was pained. "There's so much to unpack from that statement I don't even know where to start," he grumbled.

"I want to go back to you two not having sex," Rusty prodded. "What's up with that? Do you need a prescription?"

Gray cuffed the back of his brother's head, which caused Carrie to giggle. His gaze was clear when he focused on Hali. "I don't want to be pack leader. Why do you think otherwise?"

"I don't know." Hali shifted on her chair, uncomfortable. "You have powerful leadership skills, Gray. Just because I've never known you to be part of a pack, that doesn't mean you don't deserve to give it a shot. If that's what you want, I mean."

Gray was dumbfounded. Rather than approach Hali about it, however, he focused on Rusty. "Did you put her up to this?"

"Of course not," Rusty replied. "I haven't talked to her about it at all ... but only because you have her locked away in your non-love dungeon. That was a lot more hot when I thought you two were constantly getting it on by the way."

"She's getting over surgery," Gray snapped. "We get it on constantly when she's not getting over surgery. Good grief." He seemed to realize what he'd said when it was too late to take it back. "That came out wrong."

Even Hali was amused by his pout. "It's okay, baby. We're going to get it on tonight." She patted his hand.

"I don't even understand how this conversation is a thing," Gray complained. His attention moved to Carrie.

"Actually, I *do* know how this conversation came to be. You're to blame for it."

Carrie was the picture of innocence. "What did I do? This isn't my fault."

"It's totally your fault, and you know it." Gray was having none of it. "Just ... stop. You stop too," he said to Rusty when his brother opened his mouth to add something witty to the conversation. "As for the pack... Hali, I don't think you understand what an undertaking that would be."

"I understand," Hali argued. "I don't want you to say no because you think it will be too much for me, though. That's not fair to you ... and I'm tougher than I look."

"You're as tough as they come," Gray agreed. "Being pack leader has never appealed to me, though. Would I like to make sure the pack stays on the right track and doesn't devolve into madness again? Yes. I don't want to be the one in charge of that, though."

"That's why you should be in charge," Rusty argued. "You have the temperament for it. You won't fight just to fight."

"Except it would be a fight," Gray argued. "All those old-timers would insist on holding up the old ways, and I'm not okay with that."

"If you're worried about them disliking Hali, I don't think they will. She's powerful. She might not be a shifter, but she's still a badass."

"I'm not talking about this with you." Gray was firm. "It's not happening. Russell has been taken into custody. Now he's their problem." He turned to Hali for backup. "We already have a plan for moving forward. I'm going to get an office here. Right?"

Hali nodded. "I just want you to be happy."

"I'll be a lot happier when people stop thinking I want to be a pack leader."

"There's another option," Carrie offered out of nowhere.

All eyes turned to her.

"Maybe the days of needing one leader are over," Carrie suggested. She wasn't one to back down once she got started, so she pushed forward. "Having one person in charge always leads to corruption. There's no getting away from it. What about a council instead? You could be one of the council members."

Gray snorted.

Rusty, however, leaned forward. "Now that right there is an idea."

"Oh, right," Gray scoffed. "Like the elders are going to agree to that. There's no way."

"They don't have a choice," Rusty replied. "Things are already different. I like the idea of a council."

"Then perhaps you should be on it," Gray shot back.

"Maybe I will. We can be council brothers. You know, total badasses. We can wear matching T-shirts to the meetings."

Gray slid his eyes to Hali. "Do you believe this guy?"

Hali hesitated. "Actually, I don't think it's the worst idea I've ever heard," she hedged. "I can't see you taking on leadership duties, but if you were one of say seven or so, maybe that wouldn't be so terrible."

"Seriously? I..." Gray trailed off and cocked his head. It was as if his entire train of thought had been interrupted. Slowly, he lifted his chin and looked toward the beach.

"We're no longer alone," Rusty intoned.

Hali had already figured out that part herself. "How many?"

"Two," Gray replied. "They're coming in at the same time."

Hali straightened on her chair and dropped the bag of ice on the table as she prepared herself. "To be continued," she said pointedly to Gray.

"I think we're done, but we can fight about the conversation being over later," Gray agreed.

Angela was the first to come through the palm trees. She was dressed in simple shorts and a T-shirt, nothing too fancy, and her hair was shorter by a good three inches than when Hali had seen her last. Her eyes glittered in the limited light offered on the patio, and her smile was feral.

"This looks like a good time," she said.

"It is," Hali confirmed. "We're having a great time. Would you like to join us?"

"I think I'll stay over here." Angela's eyes bounced between faces but lingered on Gray. "It's nice to see you again."

Hali felt the woman reach out to test Gray with her magic. It wasn't hard, especially with the rune gripped in her hand, to slap back the effort. She watched with satisfaction as Angela frowned.

"You should probably sit so we can have a conversation," Hali offered. "That table over there is fine." She gestured toward the table closest to Angela. "I don't know if it's your sister or Regina you have with you, but they can sit too."

Angela's shoulders jerked. "What are you even talking about?"

Well, that answers that question, Hali internally mused. "I have a theory about what went down when Seth Rochester died," she started. "Would you like to hear it?"

"I didn't kill him," Angela insisted.

"Technically, that might be true," Hali said. "You were working with the others to rip him off, though. You all plotted to kill him together. So, if Regina or Cammie were the ones to kill him, you were still part of it."

"Is that what you think?" Angela turned smug.

"That's what I think." Hali took a sip of her cocktail. It was still cold, but it wouldn't stay that way much longer.

"And how did you come to this conclusion?"

Hali could sense the frustration rippling beneath Angela's surface. She'd tried two more times to tag Gray with her magic. Each time she'd been thwarted. That meant Angela was slowly realizing that she was no longer on an even playing field.

"Well, I had a very enlightening conversation with your grandmother this afternoon," Hali replied. "She's a nice woman. I have it on good authority she wasn't always a nice woman, though. She seems to have a lot of regrets."

"Oh, I bet she does," Angela growled. "What did good old Nancy have to say?"

"That she was too selfish to take you and Cammie in when you were younger. Had she, maybe you wouldn't have turned out the way you did. I almost believed Cammie by the way. She manages to pull off that whole earnest thing better than most. When I sat back to look at what I was dealing with, though, I realized that Cammie's story didn't quite hold up."

"I don't care about Cammie's story," Angela spat.

"She's here. She's over there." Hali let loose a vague gesture. "I just can't decide if she's here to end you or help you because you managed to track her down and threaten her."

"I'm innocent," Angela snapped. Her magic zinged out, this time heading for Rusty.

Hali easily batted it back.

"How are you doing that?" Angela hissed. She stalked three steps forward, earning warning growls from Gray and Rusty in the process.

"Oh, sit down, dogs," Angela seethed. "Nobody is talking to you."

"I'd be very careful right now if I were you," Gray warned. "I owe you."

Angela giggled like a loon. "You are nothing. I'm only here for your witch. I don't care about you."

"You care about him enough to use him as leverage against me," Hali countered. "In case you're wondering, that's how I truly knew you weren't innocent. Part of me wanted to believe you were some wrongly convicted woman. That by helping you, I was ultimately doing the right thing.

"After meeting your mother, I really did think you were innocent for a little bit," she continued. "When I started breaking things down, though, I recognized that wasn't true. It was honestly Cammie's choice of profession that put me on the right track, though. Then realizing Regina was also magical and was trying to fly under the radar, well, that was the final piece of the puzzle."

"I didn't kill Seth," Angela spat. "Why should I be serving time for a murder I didn't commit?"

"But you helped plan it with your sister and Regina," Hali argued. "You might not have stabbed him yourself—I'm guessing, since he was stabbed in the back—that you're the one who distracted him while your sister did the deed. It's your sister who you're most mad at, right?"

"She abandoned me," Angela replied. "We were supposed to be a team."

"But were you? Cammie got the better upbringing. Your

mother made sure of that. Cammie lucked into people who actually cared. Not that it did her much good." Hali turned her eyes to the right and was gratified to find Cammie emerging from the shadows. "Ah, there you are. I figured you would show up as well. I just couldn't decide if you made another deal with Angela, or if you were coming here to kill her."

Cammie glared daggers into Hali but didn't respond.

"If you want my take on the subject, I believe that Cammie struck another deal with you, Angela, but she's ready to run and feed you to the wolves—so to speak—the second the battle starts," Hali continued. "She doesn't want to fight you. She doesn't want to save you either."

Angela's eyes snapped to Cammie. "That's not true, is it?"

"Of course not," Cammie replied. "She's just making that up to save her own skin."

"Why would I make it up?" Hali asked. Her tone was utterly reasonable, even as she remained coiled and ready to strike. She wouldn't allow either of these women to hurt the people she loved. "You guys are outnumbered. Even if Regina shows up—and I'm guessing maybe she decided to run after all since she's not here—you're still outnumbered."

"Not if we take your men for our team," Cammie fired back. "We're stronger than you."

"You're going to take our men, huh?" Hali was feeling emboldened. "How are you going to do that?"

"We have magic you can't even fathom," Cammie replied. "It's the sort of magic that someone like you—a rule follower—could only dream of."

"I've seen that magic in action," Hali confirmed. "Your sister used it that first night. You won't be using it again."

"Is that so?" Cammie faced down Hali. "Kill her," she ordered out of nowhere. Her magic was aimed at Rusty, not Gray. Hali figured that was a strategic move. "Wrap your hands around her neck and squeeze the life out of her."

Rusty glanced over his shoulder and then at Hali. "Is she talking to me?"

Hali nodded. "Yes. She's trying to use her magic on you. She's not very good at it, though. I'm thinking she was basically a one-trick pony. She and Angela only focused on their mind magic. Cammie here doesn't even realize that she can't use you yet. Her magic isn't connecting, but she doesn't understand the hows and the whys."

"My magic is connecting," Cammie insisted. "I just haven't pulled the trigger yet." As if to prove it, she flung more magic at Rusty. This time when Hali deflected it, she sent it toward Angela.

Angela felt her sister's magic ruffle past her, and when her dark gaze landed on Cammie, Hali recognized that her group was no longer in any danger. The two sisters would destroy one another ... because that's what they were always meant to do.

"Are you stupid or something?" Angela demanded of her sister. "Do you really think that's going to work on me?"

Cammie, who had no spatial reckoning when it came to magic as far as Hali could tell, made a face. "What are you talking about? I didn't do anything to you."

"I felt it! You're trying to take me over. Why would you possibly think you could do that? You said you regretted what you did."

"I do regret it ... kind of." Cammie looked caught. "Listen, don't stand there and pretend that you wouldn't have done the same thing if our roles had been reversed. It's every witch for herself when the cops come calling. That's always been the rule."

"You're the one who stabbed Seth, and I went to jail for it!" Angela's eyes were on fire, she was so furious.

"You were standing right there," Cammie hissed. "It's not as if you weren't a part of it."

"I didn't actually do it. You stabbed him. You stole the drugs. I went to jail ... and you didn't even visit me. Where was my commissary money?"

"Oh, like I could risk that." Cammie threw her hands into the air. "If I would've visited you, then you would've seen to it that I ended up in the cell next to you. Don't pretend you weren't plotting payback. You were just waiting for a way to convince someone that I was the guilty party." She jabbed a finger at Hali. "That's why you went after her in the first place. Don't deny it."

"You stabbed him!" Angela shrieked. "I was just standing there, minding my own business, and you stabbed him."

"You were right there with me."

"And yet I'm the only one who went to jail."

Hali was expecting it, and yet when Angela threw all of her magic at Cammie, she was still caught off guard. "Holy crap!" She fell out of her chair, on her hip, and the air was knocked out of her lungs.

"Are you okay?" Gray was next to her, his attention solely for her, in a split second. "I didn't realize you were going to fall." He looked anguished.

"You can't anticipate everything," Hali pointed out. She ruefully rubbed her hip. "It feels okay. It wasn't a hard fall. We were on the sand for a reason."

"Still." Gray made a face when Rusty and Carrie

appeared under the table with them. "What are you guys doing?"

"Well, I thought we would just wait until one of them either knocks out or kills the other, then we'll handle cleanup," Rusty replied. He'd thought ahead and grabbed his drink. "They don't seem to have a lot of magic."

"They don't," Hali confirmed. "They have just enough to be a nuisance. Their mind magic is strong, but I think it's only that way when they point it at one person. Like ... they can't harness both you and Gray at the same time."

"Ah." Rusty nodded in understanding. "It makes sense. They each only went for one of us at a time."

"Yeah." Hali cocked her head and peeked out from beneath the table. Angela and Cammie were still screeching at one another. "Do you think Vin is still out there?"

"He is," Gray confirmed. He held up his phone. "He's getting bored. He says if they don't kill each other in the next two minutes, he's going to do it. I think he might have a date."

Hali was intrigued despite herself. "What makes you say that?"

"He said he has plans."

"Well, I can't wait to meet his mystery date." She peered out again. Cammie was on the ground and Angela was advancing on her. "We'll let Angela knock out Cammie. Then we'll handle Angela. Then we'll get Andrew out here to take them both in. After that, I believe we have an evening of romance in front of us." Her gaze was pointed when it landed on Gray.

The sigh he let loose was long and drawn out. "Fine. I'll have sex. Just know I'm doing it under duress. I would rather wait until you're a hundred percent."

"You're such a wuss," Rusty complained.

Hali ignored him. "I might never be a hundred percent. That doesn't mean I'm not ready to cut loose a little."

"See, I told you that you were wound too tight," Carrie said. "If you're not careful, you'll end up like those two." She poked her head out from under the table. "Oh, Cammie is down. Angela looks as if she's about to fall down. Vin has her, though. He's going to...yup...she's down too."

Hali nodded. It was pretty much what she expected. "That leaves Regina."

"She'll have run," Gray said. "She was found once. She won't risk it happening again. She won't stay in this area."

"Yeah." Hali slid her hand into his. "We'll still tell Andrew about her part in everything. It can't hurt to warn others. Just in case."

"Just in case," Gray agreed. He leaned in and rubbed his nose against hers. "This was kind of nice, huh? All we had to do was some trash-talking and they beat themselves."

"It was nice," Hali confirmed. "We're still not done talking about the council thing, though. I think it's a good idea."

"I don't want to talk about that tonight."

"Oh, you're going to be focused on me tonight. Tomorrow is another day, though."

Gray captured her chin in his hands and kissed her. "I want to focus on you for the rest of my life, so I'm good."

"I'm seriously going to gag," Rusty complained. "What is wrong with you?"

"You're the one sleeping with Hali's grandmother," Carrie shot back. "What is wrong with you?"

"Ha!" Rusty pumped his fist. "I knew you were jealous."

"Yeah, yeah, yeah. You keep telling yourself that."

19
NINETEEN

The cleanup on the beach didn't take long. Both witches were down and out, so cuffing them wasn't difficult. Hali and Carrie cast quick binding spells on them. Even though their magic was weak, it was better that they couldn't use it where they were going.

Then, still joshing one another, Rusty and Carrie took off down the beach, leaving Hali and Gray to enjoy the night.

Gray ran back to the villa long enough to grab a canteen and a blanket. Hali mixed something potent to put in the canteen. Then they headed down to the water to relax.

"What are you thinking?" Gray asked when her head leaned against his shoulder. His kiss to her forehead was as soft as the breeze.

"I'm thinking that I'm happy."

"Were you not happy until this moment?"

"No, I was. It's just ... the merrow are gone. We had another fight, and it went fine. Actually, it was almost anti-climactic how easy that was. Russell is in custody. My hip is getting better."

"Crap. I should've brought ice for your hip. I can go back and get some."

Hali glowered at him. "Don't push it."

He smirked. "Fine. I won't push it."

"You know, even when my hip aches now, it's not the same as before. That pain ... well, I knew that pain was never going to get better. It was just something I was going to have to live with. This pain is different. It's the sort of pain you push through because you know there's a rainbow on the other side."

"A rainbow, huh?" Gray chuckled. "Since when are you an optimist?"

"I think it might be you."

"I'm not an optimist."

"But you are. A pessimist wouldn't sit around thinking that we need a yard for kids that are years down the road."

"I just want my life to be with you."

Hali reached over and took the canteen from him and sipped. "Do you think your brother and my grandmother are really ... doing it?"

"I think it's cute that you refer to it as 'doing it' even though you're an adult."

"You didn't answer my question."

Gray took the canteen back and drank from it. He seemed to be giving the question a lot of thought. "I think that your grandmother and my brother like pushing the envelope," he said finally. "They like to surprise people. That's their favorite thing in the world to do."

"And?"

"And I think they probably did it."

Hali's stomach rolled. "I was afraid you were going to say that."

"I also think there's mutual respect there and it's not

going to be an ongoing thing. Your grandmother is not going to tie up my brother in a romance that's going nowhere. It might be good for him to learn from her for a bit, though. He needs to be brought down a peg or two."

"I just don't want to see it."

Gray choked on a laugh. "I don't think they're going to do it in public."

They sat in silence for a bit, content. Then Hali rocked the boat because she couldn't help herself. "Don't dismiss the idea of a council just yet. Even if you don't want to be on it—and I think you would be good in the position—that doesn't mean it's not right for the pack. They need some help."

"They do, but I can't imagine them agreeing to a change like that."

"Just think about it."

"This stuff with Russell is going to be playing out for a bit yet," he said. "He has the money for the pack hidden away somewhere. He's not going to volunteer that information, because as soon as he does, he knows they'll likely kill him."

"You don't think he'll be able to worm his way back into the leadership role, do you?"

"No. I think they'll kill him long before then."

"But?"

"But I think he can still do some damage."

"I was afraid you were going to say that." Hali took the canteen again. She was more than happy to get buzzed. "I'm going to call Cecily tomorrow about your office. Do you have any preference for what building it's in?"

"Not the main building," he replied. "I know that's the nicer building, but I'm fine with the older building out by the pickleball courts. There's a separate parking lot."

"There's also a tunnel from the far end of that building that leads to the tiki bar. That will cut down on your travel time when you want to check on me but pretend you're not checking on me. Fancy that."

He grinned. "I'll try not to cramp your style."

"Since so many of your cases overlap with stuff here now, it's a smart move," Hali assured him. "We can have lunch together sometimes."

"Not all the time, though. You and Carrie have lunch together several times a week. That's your special time."

"And it's your special time with your brother."

They drank to fill in the silence. Gray's hand moved over her back.

"Are you going to forgive your mother?" Hali asked out of the blue.

Gray was exasperated. "Seriously? You're just not going to let it go, are you?"

"No. I'm also going to keep asking uncomfortable questions until you follow through on the sex."

"What is it with you and the sex? It's not as if we're animals."

"No, but I want our normal lives back. I'm talking about all of it. It's okay that we were being careful. I'm ready to be less careful now, though."

"Your hip isn't fully healed."

"And it might never be. It's still better than it was." Hali flopped back on the blanket. "We're either going to talk about your mother or get to the romance. Which do you prefer?"

"Oh, see, this is a very uncomfortable conversation."

"We've already talked about my grandmother and your brother doing it. How much more uncomfortable could it get?"

"Fair point." He leaned in and gave her a soft kiss. "I'm thinking it's time for romance."

"Here?" There was a dare in Hali's eyes.

"Well…" Before Gray could answer, Hali's errant familiar showed up. Wayne had been flitting around the beach and avoiding the villa for the better part of the week, and when the flamingo flopped down on the blanket next to him, it was impossible to miss the smell of bourbon wafting off the bird. "We're not getting romantic with him here."

Hali made a face and focused on Wayne. "Where have you been?"

"At first I was playing house with two nice females down the way." Wayne jerked his head down the beach. "Then I got distracted."

"By prisoners?"

"No, but I saw a few of them. They seemed in need of companionship. I provided what I could."

Hali made a face. "You're really gross."

"I live my life how I want to live it," Wayne replied. "You've been busy with your own stuff. It's not as if you need me."

"Not even a little," Hali agreed. "I keep trying to send you back to my grandmother, but she won't take you. It seems I'm stuck with you … so if you want to take off for a few days, keep at it. The villa has been quiet."

Wayne rolled his eyes. "Did I ever tell you about the time I quit my last warlock?"

"Yes, and I don't want to hear that stupid story again. Find another."

"Okay, here's another one." Wayne smiled. Or whatever the approximation of a smile was for a flamingo. "There are at least twenty shark shifters hanging in the surf just outside the protective net for the hotel."

Well, now he had Hali's full attention. "What are they doing?"

"Nothing yet, but they're going to be coming to shore soon. I heard them talking."

Hali flicked her gaze to Gray. "What do you think that means?"

"I don't know," he replied. "It might mean nothing."

"It could mean something, though."

"It could." Gray stared at her for a beat, then exhaled heavily. "That seems like tomorrow's problem. I believe we have romance on the menu for tonight."

"That we do." Hali giggled when he stood and leaned over to pick her up. He threw her over his shoulder like a Neanderthal—something she didn't mind—and grabbed the canteen and blanket. "What are you doing?" she asked when she was reasonably assured she could speak without breaking out into fits of laughter.

"I'm taking you home for romance like I promised. As for you..." Gray trailed off as he regarded Wayne. "See what the sharks are up to and get back to me."

"And what will I get in return?" Wayne challenged.

"I won't feed you to the sharks when they come to shore. How does that sound?"

"Like very little reward."

"Figure it out." Gray turned and headed toward the villa. "Don't come home late and be loud either. I plan to sleep well tonight."

"*We* plan to sleep well," Hali corrected.

We. The one word made Gray go warm all over. "We plan to sleep well tonight. Try to stay out of trouble."

Wayne made grumbling noises, but Gray didn't stay to

listen. If trouble was coming—and it seemed it always was—then they would figure it out together. That's when they worked best.

"So, shark shifters?" Hali asked as Gray carried her home.

"That's tomorrow's problem, baby. Tonight, it's just you and me."

"That's exactly what I wanted to hear."